PEARLS
FOR
Prosperity

A Journey to Wealth

K.S. DWYER

outskirts
press

For Shawnae, the inspirational tide that lifts my vessel.
With my infinite love, always.

To my sister and brothers, who walked through the
Himalayas of life with me. We are forever bonded.

TABLE OF CONTENTS

Again, the kingdom of heaven is like unto a treasure hid in a field; the which when a man hath found, he hideth, and for joy thereof goeth and selleth all that he hath, and buyeth that field.

Matthew 13:44

PREFACE

I TRULY BELIEVE THAT K.S. DWYER COULD NO MORE HAVE KEPT HIM-self from writing this book than he could stop himself breath-ing. Beyond a calling, writing and sharing the wisdom in *Pearls for Prosperity* has simply been a way of life for K.S. Unique among the business leaders with whom I have collaborated, K.S.'s work is incom-plete unless he has shared it with others and helped them to pursue their own version of success – however they might measure it.

To that end, *Pearls for Prosperity* is not a how-to book; it is not simply a prescriptive road map for achieving financial or economic success. It is, in fact, much more; a means of finding one's true north and learning to rely not just on financial forecasts and markets, but on intuition, faith, providence, and trust in one's own abilities.

Above all, it is about being true to one's self and using that truth to steer us through every storm and toward every success.

It has been my distinct pleasure to lend my editorial services to *Pearls for Prosperity* and it is my fervent hope that K.S.'s treasure map – for that is what this book truly is – will help you to find the treasure you seek and to learn something about yourself along the way.

Kristen Weber

INTRODUCTION

CHRISTIAN DROVE SLOWLY ALONG THE WINDING COASTAL ROADS. He always appreciated his yearly check-in with Edwin, whose accounts he managed, because Edwin was generous and kind but mostly because he always treated Christian to lunch at Café Ostar, a stunning brasserie modeled on Casa Botin in Madrid and nestled along the banks of a brook just off the beach. The proprietors of Café Ostar had done their homework, using rounded brick archways and terra cotta floors. Most spectacular of all was the wood burning bread oven that burned both day and night, baking bread for the restaurant. Just thinking about the warm, crisp rolls that emitted tiny puffs of steam as you tore them open had Christian salivating as he parked. He could smell the baking bread before he even got to the door. He took a deep breath. The cardamom aroma mixed with the smell of the salt air and the subtle sound of the brook behind the restaurant created something unique; a sense memory that Christian would always associate with this place.

As Christian opened the door and walked in, he looked through to the back of the café to the patio sat outside, adjacent to the brook. It was a gorgeously crisp fall day and Christian saw Edwin seated at one of the patio tables. Christian indicated to the hostess that he was meeting someone, and walked through the restaurant, taking in the delicious aromas as he went. Walking through the patio door, he approached Edwin's table, a smile on his face. Christian looked around, taken, as always, by the humble grandeur of the simple setting. The leaves were deep into the throes of their autumn transformation, ablaze in fiery reds and golden umbers. Periodically, a maple seed – what he'd always called a "helicopter" since he was a kid – fell softly twirling to the ground. He couldn't imagine a more idyllic setting.

Edwin, upon seeing his colleague, stood and offered Christian a hug. This had always struck Christian. Most people in business wanted to keep things strictly professional. They were warned not to get too personal with clients or colleagues as it could cloud your judgement and make it difficult for you to act in your own best interest in the event that difficult decisions needed to be made. But Edwin had never operated that way. He delighted in the personal, always asking after one's family and health and genuinely caring about the answers. He remembered whose son was playing second base for his Little League team and whose mother had recently had hip surgery. He had never been solely about the bottom line and his heartfelt concern and kindness had certainly not hindered him in his professional life. Edwin was extremely successful; he wanted for nothing and Christian had always viewed him as someone who had it all together. Christian relished these yearly discussions because he saw them as an opportunity for learning.

"Christian, my friend!" Edwin said as they sat down. "I hope you've been well?"

"I have," Christian answered, settling into his seat. "And I have to tell you, I always love this place." He looked up at the patio heaters which held the chill of the November air at bay.

"As do I," Edwin answered. "Have I ever told you what the name means?"

"I don't think so," Christian said.

"Ostar means 'eternal goodness' or 'lasting prosperity'," Edwin explained. "Two things I believe in very strongly."

"And the food is great," Christian said, smiling.

"No better place to break bread than a place where they never stop baking it," Edwin said with a smile.

As if on cue, a waitress came by to place a basket of fresh, warm pita on the table next to a small dish of freshly-made hummus. While normally, Christian would not have been able to help himself from digging straight into the food, he was struck by the waitress, whom he had never seen before.

"Ocean," he said out loud, reading her name tag.

"Yes?" she answered.

Christian, unaware that he had spoken out loud, grew faintly pink. "I'm so sorry," he said, "that's an unusual name. But lovely," he added, worried that he'd offended her.

She smiled. Christian noticed her captivatingly blue eyes. They were a color he'd never seen before. Somewhere between sapphire and midnight; they looked truly infinite. Like, well, the ocean. He was enthralled. "My parents had great hopes for me," she answered. Glancing at Edwin, she said, "It's wonderful to see you again. I'll be back shortly to take your order."

Christian turned to Edwin once Ocean had filled their water glasses and left. "You know her well?" he asked.

"I've known her for a while," Edwin said. "She's much more than she seems."

"Is that so?" Christian asked. "You always do manage to find the most interesting people."

"I suppose I have a habit of looking for the fascinating in everyone," Edwin answered. "But Ocean is working here while she finishes her degree in archeology. She's truly an astounding person. She's overcome a great deal and faced a tremendous amount of adversity. Her work ethic and her curiosity are humbling. She's finding a way to follow her dreams and I admire that."

"That's wonderful," Christian said, tearing a piece of pita bread in half and dragging it through the dish of hummus. He could smell the fruity scent of the fresh olive oil and the sesame.

"Tell me," Edwin said, "what are some of your dreams?"

Christian said nothing for a moment. He thought and chewed, contemplating Edwin's question. Finally, he swallowed and spoke. "I guess I've always wanted to be successful, help my mother out, make sure I'm doing good work…" He trailed off.

"Those are goals," Edwin said. "I'm talking about dreams. Dreams are things you do without any ulterior motives, without any goals in mind, without any thought to the financial benefit. Put it this way," Edwin said, picking up his own piece of pita, "when you were eight, what did you want to do?"

"Hunt for treasure," Christian blurted out. He paused after he said it, considering, then doubled down. "Yeah, that's what I dreamed of doing. I still dream about it some days."

"Tell me more," Edwin said, sitting back.

Christian took a breath and said, "I always dreamed about going on a ship, searching for buried treasure. Real swashbuckling pirate type stuff. Or that's what I thought it was when I was little. Now, though, I still read about it a lot. I've learned about some of the science that's used, some of the technology. I've seen how some of these discoveries are found and it's really something." He realized that it might seem strange to be talking about his seemingly wild and far-fetched dreams with a business colleague whose accounts he managed. He didn't want to come off as un-serious or frivolous to someone as important as Edwin, but, well, Edwin *had* asked.

Edwin smiled. "That's exactly what I meant," he said. "I like knowing about people's dreams because I like finding ways to help them achieve them."

"It seems like you've found a way to live your dreams," Christian said.

"Well," Edwin said, between bites of his pita and hummus, "I had to make a promise to myself a long time ago and it's led me to a very fulfilled life."

"What's that?" Christian asked.

"I had to promise myself that whatever I did, whatever I was trying to accomplish, I had to pay it forward and make it easier for someone else to achieve their dream. It didn't start out big – I wasn't always as successful as I am now and couldn't always do as much – but investing in other people's dreams is the best way to achieve your own."

"I like that idea," Christian said.

"What matters in this life," Edwin continued, "is kindness, love, and making a difference. In the end, kindness and love are the *only* things that matter. That's what you remember. I like to say I've been in the Himalayas of life – extreme highs and extreme lows. However, I make it a point to focus on happiness, prosperity, love, and freedom. If you've got those things, you've got everything." He stopped and considered Christian for a moment. "You've heard people talk about living their best life?" he asked.

"Oh sure," Christian said. "Mostly in social media posts." He chuckled.

"Right," Edwin said. "I think we can't truly live our best lives unless we've found a way to help others do the same. There's no such thing as a solitary existence."

Just then, Ocean approached the table, order pad at the ready.

"Sorry to eavesdrop," she said, "but I heard what you said and I can tell you that I am living proof of Edwin's promise."

"What do you mean?" Christian asked.

"He's helping me with school," she said, smiling at Edwin. "He has no reason to. We didn't know each other when he started coming in here years ago, but he got to know me, asked me about my dreams, and got invested in me. I graduate in three months," she said with a smile.

"That's wonderful," Christian said, truly touched by his friend's generosity.

"He's a good man," Ocean said. She smiled at Edwin. "He asked what I cared about and truly listened to the answer. There are plenty of things we all think about, but there's usually one thing we can't stop dreaming about. For me that was digging up old stuff." She giggled. "Anyway," she said, "Edwin also taught me that there are ways to achieve your dreams right where you are. I didn't need to travel to the deserts of Egypt to study archaeology. I could find what I was looking for right here as long as I knew where to look."

"That's what some people say about love," Edwin said. "You can spend all your time looking for it only to realize it was right there next to you the whole time."

"I suppose they do say that," Ocean said, giving Christian a sly glance.

"Anyway," Edwin said, dismissing the comment, "invest in people, Christian. You'll never go wrong."

He picked up his menu and gestured for Christian to do the same. "Now, Ocean," he asked, "what do you recommend?"

"Definitely the special," she said. "Braised chicken with lemon, olives, and za'atar. And the chef is serving it with a challah bread pudding for dessert. Delicious!"

Edwin glanced at Christian, who nodded. "We'll have and enjoy two," he said.

1. ASK

IT WAS A REGULAR DAY AT THE OFFICE AND CLOSING TIME WAS FAST approaching. It was one of those days where I couldn't wait to take the elevator down from the corporate ivory tower and head out into the freedom afforded to me outside, in the fresh air and the warmth of the sun, with nowhere to go. I felt an anticipation of good things to come, and I wanted out. A vision of horses came unbidden to my mind. Some had caramel brown coats, others were deep chocolate, and the rest were a brilliant, bright gleaming gold. But they all had one thing in common; they were beautiful and free to roam the rangelands and see all the sights their freedom allowed. I had worked hard and smart but something was stirring in my soul; a yearning for such freedom.

As I finished up with the documents on my desk, the large hand of the clock hit seven. I heard a voice outside my office say, "Hey, Christian, it's lights out. I'm locking up." I had been up against a corporate deadline and knew if I didn't deliver in the morning, I'd have a very rough week ahead of me. I worked as the West Coast Marketing Director for a precious metals company but even though I earned a good salary and was comfortable in my life, I came from humble beginnings and had worked incredibly hard to be where I was. No one else was still in the office; but I didn't know how to leave early or leave things undone for the next day. It wasn't in my nature. If there was work to be done, I did it. Whether that meant staying late, coming in on weekends, or forgoing social engagements, that's what it took. I had sacrificed a great deal for this job, and thus far, it had been good to me. But recent rumblings about a merger had been worrying me. Rumor was that if the merger went through, relocation would be necessary. I wasn't even sure there would be a place for me in the new company but the more I thought about it, the more I realized that even if there was, I wasn't sure I was interested. Precious metals were not where my heart was. My heart lived in Southern California and the thought of relocating put a pit in my stomach. This was home. Could I really leave it?

I reached up for the brushed steel lamp above my desk and turned off the light. The whole time, I kept thinking, "another day, another dollar," and yet on this day, I felt a distinct longing for something more.

I made a beeline for the underground parking garage where my dusty blue Volvo waited for me. I noticed on this day, as I did most days, how out of place it looked next to the expensive European sports cars that were normally parked in the garage. However, I was partial to my Volvo and believed to each their own. Growing up, I hadn't had a car of my own; we had one car and it was shared by every member of the family. We kept it for as long as it ran and then would get a "new" one, though they were always used as well. We had a Volvo once that had lasted for fifteen good years. Perhaps out of loyalty, I'd bought a Volvo – my first truly new car – seven years ago when I'd started this job. It was still serving me well.

I walked to the parking space with my name on it; very few people had their own parking space with such short tenure with the company but I'd earned it during my third year due to my work ethic. Linda, the president of the company, told me that no one else had done that except the senior vice president. The remaining employees received their parking spaces either as five or ten-year tenured employees, or as a monthly bonus. I liked that I had been rewarded for my work ethic, not for simply being somewhere for a predetermined period of time. It made me feel as though I'd truly earned it.

As I opened the door to my car and climbed in, I looked over the royal blue dashboard and took a deep breath. I fastened my seatbelt and put on my favorite playlist. Music always helped me unwind. I drove down the exit ramp and into the lane that merged onto the freeway. As the music began to play, I began to unwind and relax and my mind was momentarily at peace.

Night was approaching and a beautiful sunset was on the horizon. The fast lane wasn't moving very fast and I glanced off to the west. The sky was blue; the golden rays of the sun rippled through the burnt orange and golden clouds spread out across the ocean. For a brief moment, I looked to the north where the picture couldn't have been more different; there was no shortage of smog and traffic. I turned back to the road ahead and saw that I had barely moved. At this rate, it would take me an hour and a half before I even got to my exit; then I still had to make it the rest of the way home. I listened to the song emanating from my car's speakers and I felt an overwhelming urge come over me. *How long are you going to do this?* I asked myself. As traffic came to another halt, I had a second thought: *What are you doing with your life?*

I hadn't indulged in thoughts like this since I had set some educational goals and started climbing the corporate ladder. If I hadn't set those goals, I'm not sure where I'd be right now, especially since a lot of my friends, like me, were still trying to find their passion. As to the rumored merger and relocation, a colleague and friend had stepped into my office the other day while I was working on a presentation for a client; he wanted to chat. This happened occasionally if he was looking to do some planning. He'd come in, sit down, cross one leg over the other, and ask how things were going. He seemed to consider me a sounding board, someone to bounce his concerns off and know that I always carefully considered my input. He told me that there were rumors that if the merger went through, a fair number of employees would be laid off, but others, a select few, would be given the choice to relocate and be promoted. He suspected, given my standing at the company, that I'd be one of those given the choice.

"What do you think you'll do?" he asked me.

I stopped what I was doing and thought about it for a moment. At that time, I wasn't really interested in leaving; I'd worked so hard to get where I was. Did I want to give it all up? Even though, in doing so, I had set some childhood dreams aside. I considered carefully before answering, but as soon as I spoke, I knew what I said was true. "I don't think I'll do it," I said. "I have other plans."

I thought about that conversation again as I drove in the direction of my home. *Did I have other plans? What were they?*

As traffic began to move slowly again, my inner voice spoke. *How long are you going to do this? Where are you going in your life right now?* I wiggled in my seat and turned the music up, trying to drown out the voice. I adjusted my sunglasses, looked up, and saw the next off-ramp. The sign read "Beach Cities Exit." I suddenly realized that I had worked so hard and put so much on the value in being the best at my job that it had been a long time since I had gone to the beach. The beach was one of the primary reasons I had moved here. When I was a child and through my teenage years, going to the beach had always calmed my mind and kept me grounded. It rejuvenated me physically. We didn't have much money, so we were never able to take fancy family vacations or fly to exotic destinations, but we were lucky enough to be within driving distance of the beach.

I tried to replicate the calming feeling of being near water early in my career; I would go to business events or conferences and when I had some downtime, I would spend a few minutes by the pool, but my mind was always on business. It got too hard for me to shut it off.

I looked to the west again where the beauty of the sun spoke peace to my soul in a way I hadn't felt in many years. *Why not?* I thought. I had only gone about ten miles since I left the office, so why not take the Beach Cities exit? I merged out of the fast lane and moved toward the off-ramp. But even this unplanned detour had my highly analytical mind clicking away. I figured there were plenty of places to eat near the beach where I could grab a bite. Traffic would die down and I would still be home at a respectable hour. As much as I tried to convince myself I was being spontaneous, I had a schedule and someone to get home to. Not a partner, per se, at least not in the traditional sense. I was single and unattached, except for my best girl, Sadie, the golden retriever I'd rescued a few years back. Sadie had webbed feet and had been abused by a former owner. On her right rear paw, she had only three toes. It gave her a distinct gallop to her walk but I'd grown to love it – and her – more than I thought possible. I had originally gotten her because I'd been lonely, working long hours with no one to talk to once I came home. But I soon realized that I needed her more than she needed me. I hired a dog walker to come and take her out a couple of times a day while I was working, but I lived for the weekends and the time I would get to spend with her. Like me, Sadie also loved the beach. I made a mental note to look for a piece of driftwood to bring back for her to chew on.

Finally, I exited the freeway and drove to a nearby restaurant where I placed a to-go order. The sun was still hovering over the horizon and I decided to take my food to the beach and catch what I could of the last of the day's sunlight. I received my order, climbed back in the car, and drove to the ocean.

I found a little parking spot just off the sand and rolled down the windows. I stared at the crashing surf and inhaled the salty fresh air as I finished my quick meal. I longed to have my feet in the sand. I took off my dress shoes, threw my socks on the passenger seat, grabbed my drink, locked the car, and headed for the beach. As I stepped onto the beach, the sand still warm from the sun, I heard my inner soul speak, *Thank you.* The sand gave off a golden-brown glimmer that renewed my body, mind, and spirit. With each step, I drew closer to the ocean; my feet began to relax and the rest of my body followed. My mind grew quiet. The crashing waves began to speak to me. *Why had I put this off for so long?* I began to feel the years of stress drop away. With each new white-crested wave pounding the sand, a feeling came over me that I had not felt for many years. I know associates and friends who have traveled to their favorite places: mountains, islands, and foreign countries. When they return, they would tell me about their journey; they'd give me a piece of the place they'd been to. As I began to relax, I, too, felt there was a piece of me here and somewhere else. I had lost the piece of my most cherished and valuable place that I had meant to carry with me. I began to walk closer to the waves and climbed the sandbar running parallel to them.

Looking ahead, I saw that some other people had brought fire-wood down to the fire pits. I decided to walk a little closer to the shoreline and let a little salty ocean water roll across my feet—what a cold and energizing feeling it was. As I looked at the waves and listened to them crash into one another, the almost musical rhythm brought a renewed strength of spirit to my soul. I continued walking along the shoreline, looking down, and as quickly as my feet would leave an impression in the sand, the waves would cover them up and replenish the shoreline as if I had never been there. I had walked along the shoreline for about a mile and when I looked up; only an orange glow was visible on the horizon where the sun had been. I continued to walk, and all my stressors fell away. I began to think about days past. I used to do a lot of boarding in years past. *What happened?* Just life, I guess.

I began to remember some of the dreams I had when I was young. Like most children, I dreamed a lot. Some of those dreams had already come to pass: I'd finished school, I'd gone on a date, and I'd played sports. While all those things were great, somehow I'd gotten off track of aligning my passion with my business or career. I had been raised never to turn down a great opportunity so when this job had come along, even though it wasn't what I had dreamed of doing, I took it and was determined to do it to the best of my ability.

Maybe all of those other things had led me to this point in my life. As I looked over the crystal blue horizon and drew in a deep breath – the air filled with the smell of bonfires and salty, moist air – it brought back a memory of passion from years gone by. When I was a young child, I wanted more than anything to hunt treasure. More specifically, I wanted to set sail on the beautiful seas and find a sunken treasure from years ago. I hadn't thought about this for many years.

As I stood there and watched the bonfire grow, the waves continued to roll across my feet. I stepped forward and my right foot bumped up against something in the sand. I was too relaxed to panic, and the water was too shallow for me to worry. I looked down to see what it was but it was gone. I took another step and felt the same sensation, almost as if something was nudging me and trying to get my attention. I was a little closer to the amber light of the bonfires and the moon had peaked through the clouds enough to shed some light on the water, and there it was, an oyster. Of all the things to wash up at my feet, I hadn't expected an oyster. I reached down, scooped it gently out of the salty, crisp water, and examined my find.

I carried the oyster closer to one of the fires so I could see it clearly. A few people told me they were leaving and asked if I would like to have their oceanside fire pit. I smiled, thanked them, and told them I'd put out the fire when I left. The sun had fully set and the moon lit the sky; I felt the cool ocean breeze. While the waves continued to bring peace and strength to me, I found a good-sized piece of driftwood and sat on it, my legs drawn up to my chest. The heat from the fire felt good on my feet and my face. I pulled the oyster from my pocket and thought that I had already found one treasure, what could be next? I vowed then and there that I would find a way of making my dream of becoming a treasure hunter a reality.

I made the most out of the time I had. I put some more wood on the fire and took a deep, crisp breath of the bonfire air. It was surreal. I looked again at the oyster and turned it over in the firelight, watching the flames glint off the shell. I felt a strong yearning for this to be the first of my treasure finds. I had to get back to my dream.

Dreams can impress so strong upon our souls,
the very thought helps to align our goals.

2. AND IT SHALL

THE WARMTH OF THE FIRE HAD DRIED THE BOTTOM OF MY PANTS. I could feel all the fibers of my body enjoying and reveling in the present moment. I rubbed the rough exterior of the oyster with my finger. I could not help but think of the magnificent journey this treasure must have been part of. How incredible the sights, sounds, and places it must have seen and traveled. Yes, it was a gift. Of all the times and places it could have washed up, it chose a time where I was looking for a sign to make a change. Timing is everything.

I added a few more pieces of wood to the fire, took the bottle of water out of my pocket, quenched my thirst, and closed my eyes. I took in the sound of the waves on the beach. I could hear it with my ears and feel it with my heart.

It seemed only a few moments had gone by before I found myself deep in conversation with my newfound friend of the sea.

"How are you doing?" the oyster asked. I replied that I was doing well. "Do you know why you were inspired to come back to the ocean tonight?" it asked.

"I wanted to avoid traffic," I said. "I hadn't been here in a long time."

My newfound treasure responded, "That is only a very small part of why you are here."

"What do you mean?" I asked.

"Some would say the stars have aligned," the oyster said. "How many do you see tonight?" I looked up at the sky, speckled lightly with stars, still too numerous to count. "Some would say it's your calling," the oyster said, "or a redirection to some of your life's purpose."

I ran my hand across the shell and turned my face to the sky of dark blue beauty. I knew this magnificent creature had crossed the seas and had experienced things I could not imagine. So I asked, "Why do you think I'm here?"

"What took you so long?" asked my treasure. I thought I detected a note of amusement, like a parent, patiently waiting for their child to ask the right question.

A feeling of elation came over both of us. It was as if the shell smiled when it responded to me. "You are right. I've had an incredible journey; but I am not finished. You see, I am here for your benefit and to be of service."

"What?" I asked. "Be of service in what way?"

"We are both here at this time to help each other," the oyster said. "Your ideas about my experiences and travels hold a great deal of truth. I have been on the shores of many nations. Many of my ancestors were used for walls that fortify cities and strengthen those around us, but we have had many different uses through the ages. I have been to many places and seen many faces. I have been in stormy seas. Those storms were full of waves that crushed everything in sight, but somehow, I survived. There have been waters so clean and warm, I never wanted to leave, but I carried on. There have been uninhabited islands and beauty most would never see. There has also been danger and depths from which only a divine source could raise me. However, out of that beautiful, rich journey, I arrived at this point in my life with you. I believe that it has been divine inspiration; something much greater than ourselves that brought us together. You see, I came from a great, ancient, and noble creation. The hands of divinity brought me here."

I stared down at the shell in my hand and waited for it to continue speaking.

"The hands that brought me here are the same ones that brought you to this point in your incredible journey," the oyster said. "You were brought here by those same great and noble hands. They care deeply about the path you are on." I did not know what to say, but my soul cried out that it was true. My treasure asked, "What were your dreams?"

Despite my fascination with the little oyster in my hand, I caught the use of the past tense. What had my dreams been? What dreams had I ignored or turned aside to pursue my career? What had I forgotten I wanted to be and do? This was what the oyster was asking.

I explained that some of my dreams had been simple and I had already achieved those, and some I had forgotten or felt like they were lofty or unobtainable. Still others had passed me by and were gone.

"What do you mean they are gone?" the oyster asked. Before I could explain, the response came. "You mean that you traded your other life learning experiences?"

"No," I said, I just couldn't see where the resources would come from to achieve some of the dreams I had.

"There is no reason to give up on your dreams; when you give up on a noble, righteous dream, it changes a piece of you. I know you know I am telling the truth because you have found a little piece of what you thought was lost. That is the beauty of dreams: they can be lost or forgotten, but they can always be found and renewed especially if they are part of your life's purpose."

"Wow," I replied. "What were your dreams, little treasure?"

"To see sights so beautiful that few others had seen, to wash upon the shores of many countries and places, and to learn great knowledge that I could one day share with others to help them achieve their desires and accumulate prosperity."

"Those are very honorable dreams. It seems like you have achieved and accomplished them all," I said.

"Let me ask you this," the oyster said. "The dream you felt the most passionate about—have you fulfilled that dream or made an effort towards it?"

I sat quietly and thought for a moment. I bet this little oyster already knew the answer. I responded, "What do you think the answer is?"

"Only by small and simple steps," the oyster responded. "That is how great things come to pass."

"Why?" I asked.

"Because that is why I was placed in your path tonight. Remember, the great and noble ones know what your purpose is."

"How can my dreams fulfill my life's purpose?" I asked.

"Let me answer your question with a question," the oyster began. "If you could live your dream, would the passion of your happiness radiate to everyone you know?" I thought about it for a second but did not answer. The oyster took my silence as an opportunity to continue. "You see, this is what the great and noble ones want. They want us to have happiness, joy, peace, prosperity, love, and the strength and wisdom to help one another through the tough times. Then they want us to take the knowledge and prosperity we obtain, apply it to our lives, and share it with others. This is how we gain wisdom for our next journey." I was speechless, but I could not deny the renewed feelings of joy and deepened desire I felt to live my dreams.

"Thank you," I said. It wasn't enough, but it was what I could manage.

Once more the oyster asked, "What is your dream? How can

you make it part of your life's work?"

So I answered honestly; I had nothing to fear. If anyone would understand, my oyster, my little treasure would. "From the time I was young," I said, "I wanted to sail the open seas and see uninhabited and beautiful places. Most of all, I wanted to find hidden or sunken treasure. I wanted to become wealthy and share a portion of that wealth to make a difference for good."

"You underestimate yourself," my little treasure responded. "That is a very real, noble and, more importantly, achievable goal."

"How?" I responded.

"You will need help."

"That's an understatement," I replied.

"It may be," the oyster responded. "But the help and resources are out there."

"Where?" I asked.

"You worked hard over the past few years," the oyster said.

"Yes," I agreed.

"Rather than look at how or where you worked, take the perspective that you were developing a powerful and gifted network and meeting people who may help you achieve your goals. Most everyone who has achieved their dreams knows that true success happens when dreams, people, and resources come together. In your network of individuals, there are untapped resources of wisdom and wealth."

"You mean you want me to share my dreams with some of the people I know?" I asked. "What if they laugh at me or discourage me?"

"Then they are not ready," the oyster said. "You achieve your dreams by helping others achieve theirs. Also, keep networking. You will find believers; use them to motivate you to get closer to your dreams. You never know when someone may become ready. You need to find people who have had success achieving their dreams. This, I know you can do."

"You have a lot of faith in me," I said.

My little treasure responded, "The ancient great and noble ones have greater faith in us than we have in ourselves. When we find even a portion of this faith, we can draw upon courage and strength beyond our own."

"Thank you, I needed to hear that," I said.

"We all do from time to time; it is easy to forget who we really are and what we are capable of. Take your dreams and passion and move forward with faith. Then and only then will you see the elements and divinity come together for the realization of your dreams and your perspective of prosperity."

Once again, my heart filled with gratitude. My little treasure continued, "Our time is limited; not only now, but on our journey. We should live our dreams with whatever time we have. We should also make use of these present moments where we help each other along the way." Then I heard my little oyster say, "I am finished for now. When you open your eyes, really look to your life's dreams and purpose, you will see things through the perspective of greatness."

My face felt dry and warm as I opened my eyes. The sun was coming up; the waves had calmed, and the darkness of night had lifted. I looked down at the little oyster I had picked up the night before, only to realize that the shell had opened and was dry around the edges. As my thoughts cleared, I heard my little treasure say, "Look and reach deep inside—the pearl is one of my gifts to you. Keep it with you and one day while achieving your dreams, you will understand why this gift was for you. Go ahead, do not hesitate, as this is part of my life's purpose."

I reached in with my index finger and felt a soft and warm sensation. Gently, I extracted the most exquisite blue, golden, and white-toned pearl beaming with light.

"Quickly, close my shell and set me free," the oyster said. In farewell, I heard the voice say, "You will discover hidden gifts and talents as you progress." I gracefully placed this wise creature at the edge of the lapping waves and watched as my fearless, faithful friend was carried back into the vast deep blue sea.

Noble and righteous dreams hear the inner divine voice of inspiration.

3. BE GIVEN YOU

As the golden misty rays of the sun rose on the new day, I took a moment to look out over the dark, emerald-green waters. The waves crashed close by and the white bubbles brushed the shore. For a moment, it was as if I was part of the scenery; I had a glimpse of perfection. As the sun grew brighter, I stood slowly, shook the sand from my clothes, and looked at my watch. It was a little after seven in the morning. *Where had the time gone?* I found, to my surprise, that I wasn't tired. But I *was* hungry and I had to be at a corporate meeting by nine o'clock. I looked around once again at the deserted beach, and headed to the parking lot, hoping that I wouldn't find a ticket on my windshield.

My car was where I'd left it, my socks still balled up on the passenger seat. I sat sideways on the driver's seat, brushed the sand off my feet as best I could, and put my shoes and socks on. Before I drove off, I remembered to look for a ticket; the windshield was clear. I reflected very briefly on what had been one of the most memorable experiences of my life, but before I realized I was doing it, I began to mentally catalogue the day ahead. *There's no way I can make it home to shower, change, and be back at the office on time*, I thought. I was only half an hour from the office, so I would need to improvise. One of the corporate perks I had was a gym membership. I would get breakfast, no, first I would hit the gym, take a few laps, and check to see if there was a change of clothes in my locker. *Yes, it was going to be a good day.*

When I arrived at the gym, the woman working at reception told me, "You smell like the bonfires at the beach."

I smiled and said, "One of my favorite places."

"Mine too," she said.

I opened my locker and saw that I was in luck: I had clean slacks and a dress shirt. And yet, no workout clothes. Instead, I decided that I would use the time I had to take a shower, eat some breakfast, and spend a bit more time thinking about my encounter with the oyster. Here, in the cold light of day and under the fluorescent lights of the gym locker room, I began to question if what I had experienced had been real after all. No, I was certain it had been. Well, mostly certain.

When I walked through the familiar doors of my office, it felt different. *What had happened?* I admit that over the past few months when I would get to the office, it felt like *Groundhog Day*. My zest for the place had been dissipating. I began to realize that it was inevitable; this had never been my dream, my true desire. You can only fake enthusiasm for so long, no matter how good the perks are.

But on this day, everything seemed to have a new energy. I looked at the people around me differently. My inner voice said, *You have been in the right place; you have been building friendships and a very powerful network. Time to use that to do what you've always wanted.*

I went into my office to pull the documents together for my presentation. I put a little music on to center myself. The radio host was giving the coastal weather report and the high and low tides. I realized after a moment that I was actually listening; it wasn't just background noise. I was taking in the words that were being spoken and internalizing them. I was totally in the moment! It was music to my ears in a way that was different than I was used to when I had seemingly thousands of thoughts running through my mind competing for attention. I was focused; I was dialed in.

When nine o'clock came, I met with my clients in the boardroom. My energy must have been contagious; things went better than they had gone in a long time. There was even some laughter, which was not part of my normal presentation. The deal was done, and the clients were very happy, as was the company. It was a win-win!

After the meeting, it was lunchtime and for the first time in a long time, I decided to take my computer to the park and eat my lunch while conducting some research on undiscovered treasures.

Normally, I ate my lunch in my office at my desk while putting together my next presentation or making notes for an upcoming client meeting. But on this day, I thought I'd spend some time thinking about my dreams, not simply my job. It felt good to connect with nature again.

As I sat at one of the many picnic tables in the park, I clicked through pages and pages of historical treasures that had been lost, as well as a few articles about unfound treasures. The energy I felt began to increase, and I bookmarked the treasures I thought I might have a chance of actually finding. I pictured myself on a ship, somewhere on an endless expanse of cerulean blue water, hunting for lost treasure. I could almost feel the wind in my hair and the sun on my back.

I hurried back to the office with more excitement than I had felt in years. I looked over the balance of the day's appointments, glanced at the clock, and put things in order to finish the day. Finally, I'd reached the end of another day of work. Down the elevator to the parking structure, then to my car. I climbed in and was on my way home. What a great day! I was energized, alive. It wasn't the presentation that had done it – though that had gone well – but rather the time I spent thinking about treasure hunting and dreaming about being outside, out of an office, out of a suit, and out of the confines of the corporate life I had been leading for so long. *I won't relocate*, I said again to myself. *It's time to do something I've always dreamed of.*

When I pulled into my driveway, I saw Sadie in the living room window, standing on the couch – where she was not supposed to be but where she was every day, without fail – and wagging her tail when she saw me. As I absorbed her happy barks and licks, I felt my mind winding down and I began to think about the events of the past couple of days. Then I heard that inner voice again: *The ancient great and noble ones have greater faith in us than we sometimes have in ourselves.* I knew this was certainly the case with me, and I wondered how I could go about increasing my faith in myself. The answer came shortly after I changed out of my work clothes, had dinner, and sat quietly in the moment, Sadie curled at my feet. *The answer you seek,* the inner voice impressed, *is to move in the direction of your dreams. Your faith will increase because you believed that you had the faith to move forward.* In other words, have the faith to keep moving forward.

Rather than my usual nightly routine of watching the television until I was tired enough to sleep, I continued researching other sunken or unfound treasure sites. What an awesome evening! I really enjoyed the time reading and researching a passion I cared so deeply about. There were a lot more treasures than I had ever imagined. That is the beauty of dreams; when we have the faith to move forward, we are met with abundance.

Over the next days and weeks, I noticed that with each new day, I grew more and more excited. The production at my office for our region also had increased. Some of my friends and associates even commented on it. They asked about my newfound enthusiasm, but I only told them that I was spending some time doing things that were bringing balance into my life. One associate said, "I noticed you get done in four or five hours what takes others eight or nine." He said that long hours, although sometimes necessary, never really impressed him, but results did. Then he looked at me and smiled. "Not a bad day." I was glad that my work was pleasing other people but I knew it was due to my newfound focus. My heart was elsewhere.

It was clear that my newfound excitement was evident in many areas of my life. I had a passion inside that I had not felt in years. Yes, I had met my educational goals, as well as some business and personal ones, but along the way, I had set my other goals and dreams aside.

As the weeks went by, I reviewed my networks and compiled a prospective list of associates who might be interested in learning about my new venture. As I reviewed the prospects in my network, I was able to construct a priority list of people I believed would help me in a business venture of seeking lost treasures. I intended to share what fortune I found, so I knew that I needed those who were similarly philanthropy minded. It was time to mine the minds of my network.

It had been about eight weeks since I'd had the life-changing encounter with the oyster on the beach. Since then, my desire to seek treasure had only increased. I felt like a kid again, remembering what it was like to be this excited about something. Whenever I would feel a moment of doubt, I would take out the folder I'd compiled and review the many treasures that were out there, waiting to be found. The old adage, "A picture is worth a thousand words" held true and I would get invigorated and excited every time.

I had heard stories of actors or business people who had written million-dollar checks to themselves from a future business or career; a sign that they'd truly made it. I had even heard that some people carried the check in their backpack, purse, or wallet until they succeeded. Others put it on the bathroom mirror where they would see it as a reminder not to give up on their dreams. I think that visualization is a key to success—seeing in one's mind what can be. I had used vision boards and positive affirmation statements to achieve goals and hit targets before when I had been a student. As an executive, I knew how powerful a single picture or positive statement can be. This time, I would use them to dream. It put a smile on my face to have a few inspiring pictures and statements strategically placed around my home and on my computer and tablet.

I constantly reminded myself about my dreams by putting pictures of ships and treasures on my computer, stuck to my refrigerator with magnets, and taped to the bathroom mirror.

I kept some of the most impressive pictures in plain view. I believed visualization would play a large part in my success. I prioritized my network list and narrowed it down to the top three people I believed could provide guidance or help as I worked to open the doors to my dreams. I chose individuals who were doing what they set out to do. These individuals were well accomplished, lived balanced lives, and were extremely successful. I always felt better after spending time with them. I decided I had compiled enough information to show them what I intended to do and what my actual dreams were, as well as what I was planning to give in return. Then I picked up the phone, set the appointments with my potential angels and investors, and made sure I had a realistic business proposal for their review.

I took some time to meditate about it. As I did, I felt a peace come over me and that small inner voice confirmed, *It will be all right. What have you got to lose? You are meant to be successful and now is your time.* I wrote these affirmations down so that I could review them often. I knew it would strengthen my beliefs in myself and those around me.

The time arrived for my first meeting with Edwin, a friend and mentor. I knew he would take the time to listen to what I had to say and offer me helpful advice.

Pilots and ship captains have a checklist prior to launch or flight. I had learned in my career to take a moment and do a mental and visual run through to make sure I was prepared for the journey ahead. I took a moment to meditate, feeling a wave of confidence and peace wash over me. I grabbed my backpack, opened the car door, and headed into Edwin's office.

Faith combined with the visualization
of dreams can allow us to draw
upon the resources to success.

4. SEEK

THE RECEPTIONIST GREETED ME WITH A SMILE. I INTRODUCED MY-self and she gestured for me to take a seat. As I sat, the oyster's words came to mind: "It's your calling." A few moments later, Aaliyah, Edwin's senior assistant, looked over with a smile and said, "Edwin will see you now."

"Thank you," I said. I picked up my backpack and headed towards Edwin's office; game day had arrived. *Remember who you are,* I thought. *Take a deep breath and relax.*

Edwin greeted me with a handshake. He gestured to the chair across from his desk so I sat down and he took the chair opposite me. Here I was, with my dream and the opportunity to share it.

"What brings you here?" he asked.

"Well," I said, "I have a business proposal." I swallowed and gauged his reaction. Edwin was used to people coming to him with business proposals. He was a true mensch. "And," I continued, "I am looking for advice and help."

Edwin laughed. "You know the old saying," he said. "Advice is only worth what you pay for it."

I nodded and chuckled along.

"Show me what you've got," he said.

"What I'm about to show you has been a dream of mine since I was a child," I explained. I already knew he had knowledge of some of my business accomplishments so I wanted to explain why this meant something to me personally. This wasn't simply another money-making can't miss business proposal of the kind he was used to hearing.

"What's your point?" he asked.

I sat for a moment, surprised at his straightforward approach, though I shouldn't have been. Edwin had been doing this for a long time. He'd mentored many people and been incredibly successful. He hadn't gotten there by beating around the bush. "Well," I began, "I want to show you a short business presentation that will explain it."

Edwin smiled. "I don't have a lot of time," he said. "Please, continue. But before you do, I want you to know that one of my dreams was to do exactly what I'm doing. It took me a while to get to this point, so settle down and show me what your dream is and let's see if we can make it happen."

I took another deep breath, hoped for a positive reception, and pressed play on my presentation. I watched Edwin's eyes and body language as he watched my presentation and thought that he seemed genuinely interested. When it was over, I looked across his large, caramel-colored desk and asked him for his thoughts.

"Just a moment," he said. He stood up and stepped outside his office for a moment. I heard him ask his secretary to take care of a client. Then he took a brief phone call and came back in, offering me a cool drink. I began to wonder if he was interested at all. Then Edwin asked his staff to hold his calls and closed the door.

"Let's talk business," he said. I realized that his seeming disinterest was actually him taking care of business so we wouldn't be interrupted. He knew that in order to focus, he needed to rid himself of distractions. "If I understand correctly," he said, "what you're attempting to do is raise the capital necessary to acquire a ship with specialized equipment, hire an educated crew, and search for treasure that was lost hundreds or thousands of years ago."

"Yes," I responded. "That's right."

Edwin sat back in his chair and said, "It's either the craziest thing I've ever been approached for, or you have the gift of chutzpah. Nevertheless, it takes passion to pursue something you truly believe in. I like it." A smile crept across his face.

I wasn't sure what to say. "I appreciate that," I said. "And your time. So...where do we go from here?"

"Christian," Edwin said, "I heard the word 'we.' I like that. It shows confidence which is a huge part of the equation necessary for success. I am at a point in my life where a venture like this could prove very edifying."

I said nothing; I simply waited for him to continue.

"Christian," he went on, "I know you understand baseball and I have always appreciated the great seats and tickets that you've so generously shared with me every year. I know you know about teams and specialized talents and skills and that years of education and training go into becoming a success on the field. There are many, many ways for one to obtain success as everyone follows their own path. Are you still with me?" he asked.

"Yes," I said. "Are you saying that I need to build a team of specialized individuals all with their own talents and skills?"

"Yes," Edwin replied. "But that's just on the business side of the venture. You will need to do something similar in order to build a crew for your ship. Each of them will need their own set of skills and talents. Now, from your presentation, I can see that you have defined the business purpose of the expedition. You will need professionals to help you put together a Gantt chart and a master business plan that includes realistic capital needs and timelines. Christian," he said, leaning back in his chair and scrutinizing me, "I believe in taking a calculated risk and yes, in my younger years, a few of the deals in which I was involved were gambles, but if wisdom is knowledge rightly applied, then if you're open to it, I can help you by building your team and crew."

Tears came to my eyes. I tried not to let Edwin see how overcome I was with elation and gratitude. My soul was touched.

"I can also help," he said, "with some of the funding, and we will bring in a capitalist and the individuals needed to develop this dream into a business and try to give you the greatest chance of success."

Edwin continued as I listened. "This sort of business venture should be broken into pieces and put back together—that way the risk isn't taken on by any one individual. I say this because most people who can afford to fund such a grand business venture will not only want a piece of the action, but a return on their investment. Some may settle for one or the other, but the way you proposed it, you were offering a return on the investment. If I was a younger man, I might gamble, but since I've been working to preserve my wealth, I would only consider a calculated risk." He paused for a moment as if still considering. Edwin smiled and said, "A calculated risk could prove very rewarding."

I was very excited that Edwin was intrigued. Like me, he had come from humble beginnings and had worked extremely hard, making shrewd decisions to find himself as successful as he was. But he was also no stranger to pain. He'd lost his father unexpectedly when he was a teenager and had found himself with more respon-sibility than most people his age. He'd had to grow up quickly. He had also lost Levi, his only son, after 28 years; Levi had battled a long illness. Edwin had graduated from the school of life and had been to the peaks of the Himalayas, all the valleys, and everywhere in between. He knew what was important and how to prioritize. I knew that each experience he'd had brought real wisdom to the decisions he made and he weighed everything in terms of risk, reward, and the character of those involved. Because of this, his words carried weight and I listened as he explained.

Edwin told me the way he saw the deal was simple. If I could find a ship that could be purchased below market value, he was willing to cash it out. After all, he could keep the ship as collateral and insure it. That way if all were lost at sea, he would be able to recover at least a portion of his capital. He also told me that if we were able to buy the ship at a really great price, then it could be refinanced at a later time and perhaps even provide additional operating capital. "You'll have to raise the balance elsewhere," he told me. "Or," he said, "you could lease it, or find a short-term rental." He explained that this would cut the initial capital outlay by a large percentage. He told me that even though it would be nice to own my own ship, if the capital wasn't available, I could always acquire a ship of my own after I found the first treasure. That way, I'd have the taste of success and the drive to do more. "What do you think?" he asked.

"What would *you* do?" I asked, "If you were me."

Edwin, like he was tossing a fastball towards my bat, sent a question right over the plate. "Have you checked the current ship markets?" he asked. "I love to put money into a hard asset that has instant equity. Think about it, Christian. Look at leasebacks and private sellers and ships that are owned by financial institutions."

Edwin also indicated that an experienced ship captain and a conditional inspection would be needed if we were making a purchase and it was his capital on the line.

I replied that I had, but only for a retail purchase. I hadn't considered leasing or renting.

Edwin said, "You have some work to do." He told me to find out who would finance the type of ship I was seeking and to find as many sources as I could, regardless of the business venture. "Every successful business venture has someone who understands the markets," he said. "If there's an area in which you're not strong, you should align yourself with someone who *is*. That will increase your opportunity for real success."

Edwin told me to call the person I'd spoken to regarding ship purchases and ask to speak to whoever handled the sale of ships that had been taken back by lenders. "Collateral will be required by the lenders so you may want to check if there were any auctions that have the type of ships you're looking for," he said. Then he told me to price out the cost for leasing and renting and when I had that information, he and I would have another meeting.

Then Edwin sat back in his chair and looked at me intently. "Where are you going to find this treasure?" he asked.

I explained that I had done a lot of research over the years and had set it aside, but over the past few weeks, I had narrowed it down to three historical treasures. All of them had a lot of supporting documentation to back up their existence as well as an approximate location of where they might be found.

"Of the top three, how many have been sought before?" Edwin asked.

"All of them," I said.

"And has anyone found any indication in their searches that those treasures are out there?" he asked.

I explained that of the three, only one had produced promising results. I told him that I'd had the opportunity to visit with Clayton, the senior officer and ocean engineer, and he'd indicated that he still had all the data from the exploration voyage and that most of the treasure was sold to a few collectors and museums; the rest had gone to colleges and universities. Clayton had indicated that he felt their discovery was but a small part of what was to be found.

"And was it found?" he asked.

"Yes, some extremely rare and ancient Olmec artifacts and other valuable precious metals from the same era," I explained.

"This is your first business venture, correct?" Edwin asked.

"Of this nature, yes," I said.

"Then it's simple," he told me. "You go where gold can be found. Out of these three sites you described to me – the one that showed evidence of treasure – that's the one you should go after."

I felt peace in what he said.

"When was the last time someone searched for this treasure?" he asked.

"About forty years ago," I told him.

Edwin suggested that I continue to learn all that I could and that Clayton might prove to be a wealth of knowledge and that with the changes in technology and the success of the previous exploration's crew, it appeared that things were lining up to make Edwin's calculated risk a smart venture.

Edwin indicated that he felt Clayton and his crew had put the framework in place and had possibly laid the foundation for additional future success.

"Smart people build on what has already been accomplished," he told me. "You don't need to reinvent the wheel…unless it's profitable." He smiled.

"That makes perfect sense to me," I said.

Edwin looked me in the eyes. "From my years in business, I have learned that there are certain times to explore uncharted waters. My inner feeling tells me this is the time for a possible discovery. Business markets are full of stories of companies that were sold out of desperation only to have the new owners come in and make moderate changes and harvest enormous profits. It's all in the perspective, drive, resources, timing, and vision. "Christian," he continued, "we both need to dig deeper and continue to minimize the risk; further data will help with some of this. Clayton is the answer at this point. His education and real-world experience should be invaluable. Don't waste any time searching for that wisdom. If he is willing to share, you will be forever blessed."

All told, our meeting lasted about an hour. It was straightforward and Edwin didn't hold back. I appreciated his candor.

Before we concluded our meeting, Edwin took a few minutes to recap and indicated to me that if I continued to learn all that I could about the current ship markets as well as everything Clayton was willing to share with me – including the records from the previous expedition and Olmec trade routes – he had no doubt that the doors would open to a venture I had dreamed of since I was a child.

Edwin stood up and came around his desk. He opened his office door. As I stood up, he smiled and said, "Christian, you have been staying the course. I have seen a great deal of action, effort, and faith from you and these are all signs of success. You are on the right path and are no doubt passionate about the direction you are headed. Possibly you have found your life's work. Your diligence will be rewarded, I am sure of this. The stress I see on your face from the unknown status of your current employment situation will work out as long as you keep staying the course. You are not the first person to find themselves in this situation and you won't be the last. Change can be hard and you are laying the foundation to be the architect of some incredible changes rather than a casualty of circumstance."

We shook hands and I let him know how much I appreciated his guidance, time, and wisdom.

Edwin replied, "I am excited to see what comes next."

Once the door of your dreams has opened, follow through before it closes.

5. AND YE SHALL FIND

I SPENT THE NEXT COUPLE OF WEEKS GOING INTO THE OFFICE EARLY so that I could stay on top of things at work, as well as complete the targets and tasks I wanted to be well prepared for my next meeting with Edwin. I found that I was learning a lot, as I looked into the things Edwin had asked me to explore. Edwin knew what he was doing. Equally important, I was doing what I had said I would do. I believe that a person is only as good as their word, so I knew I had to hold up my end of the bargain.

The day for my next meeting with Edwin arrived and I had spent as much time as possible ahead of time gathering all the information I could. I knew that if I had more time, I could have found additional market data as well as more ship data but I was anxious to get the ball rolling. I also knew that while research and doing one's due diligence were important, inertia is a powerful force to overcome. I wanted to capitalize on the momentum I was feeling to go after my dream.

Once again, I arrived at Edwin's office and when he was ready to see me, I was greeted with a smile, a handshake, and a formal business hug, and invited to sit in the familiar chair.

This time, however, Edwin asked his secretary to hold all his calls, and then shut the door. "How did the last few weeks go?" he asked.

"I felt as though I'd taken an exploration voyage but never left the shore," I told him.

Edwin chuckled. "You're learning your market, learning the way of success," he explained. "I never venture into business deals for which I don't have the most current market data or research. Remember this now and in the future. Let's go over your findings."

"The ship markets are soft due to the recent global economic slowdown, and the ship brokers I had an opportunity to speak with all indicated they had plenty of inventory, and the financial institutions and auction houses all confirmed they do as well. There are ships available for pre-purchase inspections," I explained. "Some auction houses and ship brokers said they would waive a lot of the fees to put a deal together. I spoke with a couple financial and economic advisors in this field and they said the ship market could possibly drop lower, but that I shouldn't quote them on that."

Edwin nodded, waiting for me to continue.

"One common thread," I said, "was that they all agreed once the dry bulk market increases and some of the current regulatory tariffs normalize, the market will remain soft. The large ship market is hurting due to daily operation costs. The mid-size ship market, the type that we need, are in a few ports."

Edwin smiled and said he had seen this cycle before in commodities, real estate, and the stock markets, as well as other retail markets. He told me that when we understand those markets, a different kind of ship, a ship of opportunity presents itself. "Even so," he said, "What are the lease or rental markets like?"

I told him there were only a few companies that would even consider such a venture. I gave him the figures and he turned to his computer, typed for a few minutes in silence, and then turned to me and said, "This is the time to buy. The market cycle makes sense and we would be investing at the bottom of the market. If things don't go well, we could lease or rent the ship out to recover our investment. I've done this before with residential and commercial properties and other retail products over the years. When the markets strengthen, we can sell it off." He sat back in his chair. "I've done well being in tune with the markets," he added.

I got really excited; I could feel the enthusiasm in the office increase. I shared my findings; the map that had been used in the original exploration was now public record, so I was able to obtain a copy of it and had it with me. Clayton, the senior exploration engineer who had been a consultant on the original voyage was still alive and living in the Rocky Mountains. He was ninety-three years old.

"Let's call him," Edwin said.

When Clayton answered, I introduced myself and spoke to him about my idea and his experience. He shared with me that he enjoyed reading my emails and that it was nice to hear my voice. He said, "I feel my mind is still sharp. When I think about that exploration forty years ago, I get as excited now as I did then."

"Time is priceless," Edwin said. I knew, once again, he was speaking from experience. Though his son Levi had lived but 28 years, he'd spent many of those years serving a number of humanitarian missions in several north and South American countries. Just prior to his passing, he had begun playing classical music for patients undergoing cancer treatment. Edwin explained to me that a couple years prior to Levi's passing from this life into the next, Edwin had scaled down his business affairs so that he could spend more time with his son and loved ones. Looking back, Edwin said that he was grateful for that time they'd shared as a family; it had proven invaluable. I know it had given him a true appreciation for the value of time.

Clayton said he was grateful for the opportunity to answer and share any information he had. I thanked him, wished him well, and we hung up.

Edwin sat back in his chair, smiled, and said, "Nicely done, but we have a lot more to do." He nodded at the piles of paper I'd brought with me. "You're making progress."

"What do you suggest I do next?" I asked.

"Music to my ears!" he said, smiling. "Let's review the total cost."

We spoke for a few more minutes before he looked at his watch, apologized, and told me he was running short on time. "I've greatly enjoyed our time together," he said, "and I have a couple of assignments for you."

"Of course," I said, preparing to take notes.

"First," he began, "I want you to find a ship captain with experience and success in the field. After you've narrowed it down to three or four choices, bring me their credentials and I will do a review and help you make a decision based on criteria; we'll discuss it at our next meeting."

"If I knew the requirements now," I said, "It would be a smoother process."

"Not necessarily," he said somewhat cryptically. "But do the best you can."

He then asked me to obtain the lenders' current inventory list of the type of ships I thought could handle the voyage. "Some of the lenders may charge a small fee," he said, "but most of them should be more than willing to provide a complimentary ship inventory list.

"Now," he said, "What do you know about the current market value of the treasure you're looking for?"

I shared with him that the treasure pieces that had been found were in international waters and there may be some taxation if additional treasure was found. "Clayton believes the taxation could be minimized. We could lower or offset the taxation by working with colleges and universities as well as a few select national and international museums," I said. Then I told him that the combined net worth of coins, gold, and other historical artifacts was estimated in the millions, but some pieces could be of infinite worth. Whether it was the historic or financial value, I had piqued Edwin's attention.

Edwin turned to his computer, was silent for a few minutes, then looked me in the eyes and said, "Even if there's only a partial find, the reward may be greater than the risk. This is the language of success." He stood up and shook my hand. "I'll see you in a few weeks. We will discuss the rest of the crew then."

Edwin gave me a business hug, smiled, and told me it would be all right. As I headed out, I noticed every seat in the lobby was full and I realized that I had not properly thanked him for his time. I made a mental note to send him an e-mail in the morning as well as an old-fashioned card in the mail.

I was heading down the freeway when I was struck by the reality of what was happening; I was making progress toward my dream. The passion you feel when you realize you're getting that much closer to achieving your dream results in pure elation. As I listened to a favorite playlist, my mind was filled with the direction, guidance, and help I was receiving from Edwin, but from elsewhere as well. I remembered what the oyster had said; "You were brought here by those same great and noble hands. They care deeply about the path you are on." I had been told that when we really believe and have faith, we should keep moving in the direction of our dreams, and the universe will help the stars align on our path. I had also been told that faith can move mountains and, in my case, it can apparently also acquire, chart, and staff a ship! Things were moving forward and I felt all of my experiences had led me to this exhilarating place and time in my life as well as those I now had the privilege to work with.

When all of the elements of the universe combine in the direction of your success, you need to set fear aside.

6. KNOCK AND IT SHALL BE

THE FIRST THING I DID THE DAY AFTER MY MEETING WITH EDWIN was to book a flight to meet Clayton in Colorado. He was the last surviving crew member from the previous exploration and I couldn't wait to meet him in person. I had spoken with him on the phone again, and he had invited me to his home. It was such a privilege. The purpose of my trip was to gain the additional knowledge and wisdom that Clayton had amassed, both on that journey and over the course of his blessed life. I suspected that, if he were willing, he would make an excellent mentor for me.

As I finished out the week at the office, I compiled the inventory ship list from the lenders that were willing to sell. The list of captains and their resumes would be available the first part of the week and I would take that to Edwin. After work, I headed to the airport.

I was lucky enough to have seat 10A, a seat in the emergency row, which allowed for extra leg room. I had spent most of the week spending long hours at my desk both working and getting together the information I needed for this upcoming visit with Clayton and my meeting with Edwin that I realized I hadn't taken the opportunity to really stretch out in several days. I stuck my legs out in front of me, again, thankful for the extra leg room, and rotated my ankles, loosening my tight joints and trying to relax. I nestled in and got the usual instructions from the airline attendant and committed myself to helping in the event of an emergency.

The flight itself was uneventful, and shortly after take-off, I fell into a light sleep. When I awoke, I was unsure how long I'd been sleeping but the man sitting next to me must have seen my confusion as he smiled and said, "You've only been dozing for about an hour." He was a gray-haired gentleman with the wrinkles of time on his face. I noticed that he had a cane, a book, blue eyes, and a deep but peaceful voice. We spoke of the airline snacks, the weather, and the estimated flight time. I gestured to his book. "Any good?" I asked.

He smiled. "Yes, amazing" he said. "But some of the greatest joys are found on the open seas." He sounded wistful. "What do you do for a living?" he asked.

I told him that currently I was a marketing director for a firm on the West Coast, but that it looked like I'd be leaving that position soon to fully pursue my passion and going into a business venture in the near future; I did not want to elaborate until I knew it was a done deal but I was finding that I was really excited to talk about it. I'd never felt that passionate about marketing.

He smiled and said, "Isn't it a blessing to be able to do what you love?" He looked thoughtful for a moment and then continued. "My passion was the open seas. I was a captain for many years. Our ship charted many waters, national and international. I brought the old vessels through some of the worst weather imaginable and through wars in the darkest nights. Believe it or not, I have seen peaceful waters with so many colors it would bring tears to your eyes. There was one coastline where the rhythm of the waves calmed my soul after the enemy had sunk some of my friends and the ships of my fellow captains." He looked off for a moment. I could see the tears in his eyes as he was no doubt remembering that sacred time before he continued. "The water has a way of bending that which will not break. It can also take your spirit to a place that words cannot describe. I miss the sea."

"What happened?" I asked quietly.

He told me that he'd been asked to take a medical retirement because he'd been diagnosed with cancer. "I'm in full remission now," he said. "Just got a bit of a limp in this leg." He tapped his right leg with his cane for emphasis.

"What got you through?" I asked.

"I spent a lot of time in meditation and prayer," he said, "and the prayer of others gave me great strength." He told me that his doctors were excellent, but his type of cancer had a low survival rate. "But I have always defied the odds in my life, and I believe the illness gave me time to think about why I'm here. It also made me appreciate and see things from the correct perspective. I was always in a hurry and I never took the time to smell the roses. Now, I have a garden and a flower bed. I make sure there is time for joy. I've come to realize that happiness is a big part of why we're here."

This is a very wise man, I thought to myself.

"When I was sick and lying in bed, I would visualize the things I wanted coming to pass in my life as well as the things I still wanted to do. The first thing I wanted was to see myself healthy; I figured that if I got well, then I could accomplish the other things. I did still do some of the things I wanted to do while I was ill, but I kept my thoughts focused on seeing myself well. I also pictured myself with family and friends. Those were some of the people who prayed for me. There is strength in numbers. Helping other people was a lifetime dream of mine. I wanted to take some of what I'd been blessed with and share it with others. I kept the faith that one day I'd captain a ship out on the open waters once again. I have succeeded in two of those three things."

I asked him where he was headed and he replied that he was going to visit his daughter. He told me that in her kindness, she would take him for his annual checkup. Then he smiled, telling me she wanted to give thanks to some of those people who had helped him with an additional seven miraculous years.

He asked where I was going and I told him that I was going to see Clayton, a retired exploration engineer whom I hoped would share a lifetime of wisdom with me. "So far," I said, "I've only spoken to him on the phone."

"You're on the right path," he told me. With his words, I felt tingles down my spine. I told him that I appreciated his thoughtfulness and his willingness to share a little of his life with me; I told him that his timing was perfect for where I was in my own life.

"We find our true selves when we are in the service of others," he said.

After a moment of silent reflection I said, "Thank you, I will remember that."

As the plane landed and taxied to the terminal, I felt that I was a better person than I had been only a few hours before because of what I had learned listening to this wise man. When the "ding" sounded, announcing that the plane was ready for deboarding, the man stood up, stuck out his hand, and introduced himself. "Captain James," he said, "retired." I shook his hand and we wished each other well. I walked up the corridor and off to baggage claim. While I waited for my luggage to arrive, I thought about Captain James and realized that I wanted to stay in touch with him. I saw him approaching and walked to meet him.

"Would you mind," I asked, "if we kept in touch? I would love to be able to keep up with how you're doing and to let you know how my journey is unfolding as well."

"That sounds wonderful," he said, smiling.

We exchanged contact information and shook hands again, smiled, and went our separate ways. He had a ride waiting for him, and I was grabbing a shuttle bus to a hotel for the night before meeting Clayton the following morning. It was late and I was tired, but I was looking forward to the next few days.

At the hotel, the desk clerk told me that I had a message. It read, "Don't worry about trying to find my home. I will be there at 8:00 a.m. sharp to have breakfast. Your friend, Clayton." I found that despite my exhaustion, I was looking forward to it.

The next morning came quickly but I had slept well and was full of vigor. I awoke early, went for a run on the treadmill in the hotel's gym, then took a shower and was downstairs in the hotel lobby at 7:55 a.m., waiting. A gray-haired, bearded man with a plaid jacket and soft tan hat walked in shortly after I sat down. He moved a little slowly and called me by name as he approached. I stood up and shook his hand. He smiled and said that his driver was out front waiting to take us to breakfast.

I thought, *Great, it's probably a quaint little place.* But I was wrong; it was a national chain, but they knew Clayton by name and the food was great.

As we became acquainted, he asked me to call him "Clay" and he shared with me the details of his previous treasure hunting. Clay said that other than having his own family, that expedition was the greatest legacy of his life. I asked him if he had any regrets.

"Only one," he said. "I'll tell you about it later." That piqued my curiosity but I decided to let him reveal what he chose in his own time.

I learned a great deal during that breakfast about Clayton's own personal history. Aside from the expedition he'd headed, I learned that he had been orphaned at a young age and as a result, had needed to grow up very quickly. After graduating from high school, he'd enlisted in the military to serve his country. He soon found himself in active infantry and earned five battle stars including the Purple Heart for the wounds he'd received. At the conclusion of the war, he'd found himself back in school and had tested in the top ten percent. He was accepted to a top university where he'd studied engineering. Later, he worked for some of the top exploration firms in the world. Yet through it all, despite the treasures he'd discovered on his journeys, he never failed to claim that his true treasures in life were his children, family, and friends.

Clayton had copies of notes and logs that he thought might be beneficial to me and he shared some pictures and maps from the exploration as well as a copy of his own journal. He said it brought him great joy to know that someone might finish what he and his crew had begun forty years ago. Some people had said that his exploration had failed, but those same people had been negative about the trip before it had even begun. Historians had told him that the exploration had set a milestone in what they were able to find, but in reality, it had actually allowed them all to have a better life. He felt that he was successful because he had tried, and his journey had made a difference.

"Maybe you've heard this before," he said, "but it's true as sure as I'm ninety-three years old; you're never too young to make a positive change in this life and it's never too late to make a difference for good." With that, Clay ordered a refill of his coffee, smiled, and took a sip of water. "Yes," he said, a faraway look in his eyes, "there's nothing like being on the open seas. We had some challenges and setbacks, but we didn't focus on them, only on what we had to do. Besides, some of the challenges turned out to be opportunities."

"That's how I'm trying to view things," I said, thinking about my job situation and how I was attempting to turn that challenge into an opportunity.

Clay nodded and told me he wanted me to go for a drive with him. He also insisted on paying for breakfast.

"Where are we going?" I asked.

"It's a surprise," he said with a smile.

After a few minutes of driving, we arrived at what appeared to be a large warehouse. Clay gave his driver the code to the gate, and we went in. We turned left, and he told his driver to stop. Then Clayton got out and pushed a button to open the door. As the doors rolled up, I was struck speechless. There, before me, was the original ship from the first exploration. I approached it—everything appeared to be in genie condition. It was all original. Clay said, "I negotiated a deal. When I pass away, as part of my legacy it will go to a museum. Please feel free to touch it, smell it, and walk through it. This will make it real for you."

I was elated; it felt surreal. Clay took a few pictures for me. When it was finally time to go, Clayton walked over to an old relic of a desk and picked up a stack of documents and maps. He brushed some dust off them and held them out to me. "These are our copies of all the pertinent documents that may be of interest to you. I was approached a few times to share this data, but you are actually the only individual that has followed through and for that, I have a very strong feeling that you will be successful."

I took the documents and maps and held them closely, reverently. I was humbled that he had chosen to share them with me.

Clay then asked if I would mind if we made one more very important stop. "It will only take a moment," he said.

"Of course," I said. "It's an honor just to spend a little more time with you."

Clay's driver pulled up to a florist at the next corner. He motioned for me to follow him into the shop. When we entered, the woman behind the counter handed him a dozen tulips. "Your usual order," she said with a smile.

We got back in the car and set off again. A few blocks later, we arrived at a cemetery. We pulled up to what I could see was a familiar spot. My friend got out, carried the purple and red tulips to a gravestone, and set them in a water-filled vase. The lawn had been freshly cut and I could smell the spring grass. The beautiful tulips radiated with color. I watched Clay, on bended knee, remove his hat and utter a few words, then stand up and appear to regain his composure and return to the car.

"Thank you," he said, "I really miss her."

Silence filled the car for a few minutes. Eventually, Clay explained that his wife had passed three years before; they'd been the best of friends. Each Saturday, he brought her new flowers. He looked at me with tears in his eyes. "You know, towards the last few steps of your journey, the ones you love and the memories you make will have the greatest impact on your life. Make your time worthwhile."

We arrived back at the hotel, and I already felt that my life had been enriched. "When I was your age," Clay said, "I felt like time was on my side but you know none of us are guaranteed tomorrow." He also advised me to pursue my passion and enjoy my life's work. I let Clay know that I appreciated his time and wisdom and I shared with him that I'd had a few dreams of finding treasure on land.

Clay stopped in his tracks and offered me a sheepish grin. "There are islands in the area that did not show up on the maps," he said. "Perhaps one of them could prove to be the balance of the equation to success? Only time will tell. But I know this for sure, Christian," he continued, "it's important to follow your righteous desires and dreams."

"It may mean nothing," I said, shrugging, "but it may also be the rest of the equation to success."

"Follow your dreams," he said.

We shook hands and I gave him a hug and thanked him once more.

"You will find what you're looking for," he told me.

I had a red-eye flight, so I went up to my room, reviewed the information Clay had given me, and called his home and left a message on the answering machine that I greatly appreciated his friendship, time, and the information he shared. I packed my bags so I would be ready, rested for a bit, grabbed a bite to eat, and climbed on the shuttle to the airport which crawled along through the congestion of mass transit.

As the plane came in for a landing, I realized I was glad to be home. I grabbed my bags. I was determined to make my time count. I had missed Sadie and the weather was perfect for a sunset walk on the beach. I dropped my bags and backpack at the house, took one look at Sadie, and asked, "Beach?" She went bounding out the door to wait for me at the car. I locked the door behind me and followed her out.

Although I felt a little jet lagged, I was amazed at the events and information I'd learned over the past few days and couldn't wait to share my findings with Edwin. I pulled into the beach parking lot, kicked off my shoes, and tossed them in the back seat. Sadie and I set out together on the sand. Even though she has the better nose, the smell of fresh, salt air and the sound of rolling waves permeated my very soul. Sadie and I took a moment to sit and watch the golden rays of the sun pass through the rolling blue waves. A memory of the words my little friend, the oyster, had spoken to me came rushing back. "Each of us has a divine and noble purpose." I put my arm over Sadie and pulled her to me in a hug. I knew she was fulfilling her purpose of being my loyal companion on this journey.

Together we enjoyed the brilliant sunset as the sun's golden rays painted the sky in beautiful pink, orange, and purple hues. Recharged, I turned to Sadie and said, "Time to head home." She beat me to the car, her tail wagging, ever eager to see what was next.

It was unbelievable that in forty-eight hours, my life had changed so much.

We should never take our time here for granted; it is one of the most valuable gifts we have been given.

7. OPENED

I HAD A WEEK LEFT TO FIND A CAPTAIN, IN ADDITION TO MY NORMAL workload at the office. For the first task, I worked with a head hunter and conducted the interviews early in the morning and late in the evenings, before and after work. By the end of the week, I had been through a dozen different applicants. I never told them what the ship would be doing or the location we would be traveling to, only the general vicinity in which we would be exploring. I reviewed resumes, collected references, and kept my part of the conversation strictly business. I felt that if I disclosed my plans to someone whom I didn't end up hiring, it might cause future problems. As the saying goes, "Loose lips sink ships." Perhaps never more apt than when dealing with sunken treasure.

When the weekend finally arrived, I spent it unwinding and doing some of the things I had put off, remembering what my friend, Clayton had said about making my time count. I took Sadie for a couple of long walks, visited the beach again – keeping my head down and looking for my friend, the oyster – and sat outside under the stars.

The ocean was beautiful and I caught the sunset late Sunday evening. The pink and blue hues radiated over the crisp green and white water. The sky was clear and it was nice to see the many forms of wildlife. I have always felt at home when I was by the sea.

After a weekend in which I felt refreshed and rejuvenated with a renewed sense of purpose, I began Monday morning by picking up the phone and calling to confirm my appointment with Edwin. His secretary let me know that Edwin wanted to change the appointment to Tuesday, as he had just returned from a trip out of the country and he needed a little time to come up to speed on things.

"That works great," I said, thinking that it would give me a bit more time to prepare. "Would you mind if I asked where he's returning from?"

"He's been doing humanitarian work in Peru where people need help," she said. Edwin helped a lot of people in the United States, where he was born, but he also did a great deal abroad. She asked if I needed anything else.

"No, thank you," I said. "I'll see you tomorrow."

Though he was American by birth, Edwin could choose to live anywhere. However, he chose to live near a National Park because he had the utmost respect for the Master's creation and being so close to it humbled him. I appreciated that about him and how his choices always seemed intentional and not happenstance.

This was an important meeting and I felt the time had come to make a vital decision that would change things in my life and my future. On Tuesday, I finished what I needed to do at work and took an early lunch. When I arrived at Edwin's office, he greeted me at the door. He was quite tan and his spirits were high; I felt his energy. He invited me in and showed me some great artifacts he'd brought back from his trip as well as some modern cultural items he'd been given. Edwin then looked me in the eyes and said, "I never go with any intent other than to give, but the villagers outside of Machu Picchu insisted I take these. I didn't want to offend them, so I took them. It's interesting that sometimes it's more difficult to receive than to give, but they are my friends and I know we were all enriched by the experience."

"Was the trip itself a good one?" I asked.

"It was," he said. "We got a lot accomplished: we helped to make fresh water available, worked on building a new school, and delivered many donations that were needed. The young people who went with us said they were overcome with a love for the people and a love of service," he smiled. "Now, let's see where we left off. What have you done over the past few weeks?"

"After I left here," I began, "I went to the Rocky Mountains and met with Clayton, the senior exploration engineer from the original expedition voyage." I shared that I'd had an interesting flight and that I'd met the retired military ship captain, James who'd sat next to me on the plane. Then I informed him about all the additional documentation I'd received from Clayton. I shared with Edwin the additional research I'd done and brought him up to speed on how the interview process had gone.

Edwin responded, "When I went into business for myself, I had a higher purpose than merely amassing wealth. Have you thought of your higher purpose?"

I told him that in the excitement of it all, I had not spent much time thinking about what my higher purpose was. "Edwin," I said, "all I know at this point is that I would like to use the gift I have been given to make a difference for good."

"Sounds promising," Edwin said. "We'll spend some more time on this in the near future. Let me see your ship inventory list."

It felt good to hand Edwin four sheets of bank and financial institution ship inventory. He took the second sheet and said he had done business with that company before. He put a star on the top, looked at the third sheet, and threw the fourth one away.

"I have pictures and the equipment lists are on their way," I said.

"That's good," Edwin replied. "I'm glad to see you had the drive and passion to visit Clayton—that shows determination and focus. Christian, do you believe that when our thoughts are focused on the things we truly want in life that a higher power combined with the laws of the universe can make these things happen?" He didn't wait for me to answer before continuing. "And here's another question; when you harness your thoughts for good, will good come?"

"I believe in the power of positive thinking if that's what you're asking," I responded.

"Yes, that's part of it," he said. "Do you believe the life you're living is a direct result of your thoughts?"

"Yes, thoughts play a very direct role in our environment, our setbacks, and our success," I said.

"Then thoughts can attract both positive and negative things, or affect events in our lives?"

"Yes," I answered. "I believe there is a lot of truth to that."

"Well then, you're ready." He smiled.

I set the three resumes on his desk, told him about the interview process, and gave a report of my findings. Then, I waited.

He looked at me, put the resumes in a pile, and handed them back to me. "You won't need these," he said.

"Why?" I asked.

"You already have your captain," he told me. "You sat next to him on the plane."

"But you've never met him," I said. "He walks with a limp and he has some health problems and was asked to take a medical retirement. How do you know he's the one?"

Edwin chuckled and replied, "Christian, something in my gut — call it a hunch, call it wisdom — tells me that James is your captain and I feel that once you speak to him about this, you may find he has the heart of a lion, the spirit of a warrior, and plenty of wisdom and chutzpah."

I nodded.

"What have you been thinking about?" he asked.

"Finding a captain, a ship, and all the other information I could," I said.

"Then if your thoughts have been focused in this direction, why couldn't James be your captain? You don't have the time to go out into the world to look for the experience he has. The universe has brought him to you. Let's call him."

"I only have his e-mail," I responded.

He asked his secretary to come into the office. He handed her the piece of paper on which I'd written James's email. "Send an e-mail to this man and tell him it's urgent that he call Christian."

"Of course," she said.

Edwin turned back to me. "Let's move forward; once you talk to James, get his resume and references for your records. As far as I'm concerned, he's the right man for the job. He survived cancer, which tells me he has great things to accomplish. You and I will learn a lot from him. Also, he'll know which type of ship is right for handling this type of voyage. Now, I want you to start to think about the type of company you'll be setting up. I have a friend, Dwight, who's an international attorney and he's agreed to help for a deferred fee; he wants one of the first coins you find."

"What if I only find one coin?" I asked.

"You don't have to worry," Edwin said. "I'll take care of it. I also want you to start thinking about the crew for your ship. The captain will choose his first and second mate but you'll need to help with the rest. Now, you are worried that you'll only find one coin?"

I nodded. "It's possible," I said.

Edwin chuckled and said, "Christian, feed your mind abundance, prosperity, and wealth. When I founded my company several years ago, I did what I have just asked you to do. My company has not only survived, but thrived. We learned that it's all right to change and pivot to meet and address market conditions and in doing this, our products and services continue to be in high demand." He smiled. "When the recession hit for a few years, my competitors would call me and talk about the news reports and the market conditions as well as how far off their business was. I believe in staying in tune with the markets. Many companies, including mine, that are still in business focused on diversification and innovation and some technologies and a few made major changes. The companies that continued to focus solely on surviving the impending doom are no longer here."

He paused and looked right at me, "Now how does this affect you? It's very simple; as you build your company, your needs and markets will continue to change. The one constant *will* be change. As you achieve success in business and leadership, you need to be able to draw on your inherent gift of adaptability. The captain of your new ship will know this well. I believe Captain James is not only extremely gifted and skilled, but he rose to success by being able to adapt early on to war and weather conditions."

Edwin then asked, "Is there wisdom in a business person or entrepreneur adapting to economic cycles and the market and sometimes political conditions?"

Before I could answer, he said, "Of course there is if you want to survive and prosper.

"Does a successful entrepreneur adapt to economic force so that he can thrive and survive? This is a universal gift from our creator. Take the animals of the jungle; a chameleon has the ability to adapt to its environment, which has allowed this little creature to survive for millions of years. There are other gifts and talents I would like to discuss with you, but time is short. I have a couple of assignments for you if you would like to keep moving forward. But as for the captain, you know who your captain is. A divine power brought him to you."

"Are you sure about this?" I asked.

"Yes, I am. I believe you can look forward to his call."

"Thank you," I said.

Edwin sat back in his chair and continued. "Over the years, you'll see that your gut or a peaceful voice will confirm the right decision, and then your confidence will wax stronger. Talk to Dwight about your business entity. My inner voice tells me that you will be incorporating, so think of a name for your new corporation as well as a few directors, a secretary, a vice president, and a treasurer. You may fill some of these positions initially, but remember to select individuals who have gifts and talents that will enhance what you're doing. This will strengthen your company and the people will strengthen each other. I've had the privilege of surrounding myself with the type of people I call mentors. Some of them were already extremely successful, while others had hoped for the opportunity to achieve their dreams. The saying, 'No individual is an island unto themselves' is true. I've never been afraid to learn or work with these gifts. It has blessed me throughout my life.

"I've said a lot," he concluded. "What are your thoughts?"

"A lot is going through my mind right now," I told him truthfully. "Edwin, I am thinking about my call with Captain James and where that will go."

"Excellent," Edwin said. "Now, I know your next question is either about the ship purchase or company choices—your attorney will help with all the documents and paperwork. As far as the ship acquisition, I think it would be wise for Captain James to have some input into this as well. He will know the ship of choice. We can upgrade it if we choose once you and Dwight and James have finished your discussion. I will await your next visit. I would like you to think about a few gifts with which I have always tried to surround myself. By that, I mean individuals who reflect these character traits, people who, over the years, have made a positive contribution to my company. These gifts are honesty, integrity, and making a difference for good. Remember also as you move forward that if you have moments of doubt, think of all of the opportunities that have brought you this far. 'The earth is full and there is enough to spare.'"

Once again, I thanked Edwin and let him know how much I appreciated his time and mentorship. We shook hands and he gave me a business hug; I could feel his sincerity. "You never know what's possible until you try," he said. "Christian, it appears you're on the right path."

Abundance, prosperity, and wealth. And to think, a respectful and simple conversation on a plane could lead me to finding an amazing leader and ship captain. Things were about to get really interesting.

Find mentors who impart righteous wisdom,
for great and valuable wisdom comes at a price.

8. UNTO YOU

AFTER RETURNING HOME FROM THE OFFICE, I TOOK A MOMENT TO ponder and visualize all the essentials I would need to make my dream come true. As I was settling into my evening, my phone rang; it was Captain James. I explained the unlikely and serendipitous opportunity and he jumped at the chance. Edwin had been right; James wanted to be part of the mission. He talked about how there are times in each of our lives that, if we're open to it, our infinite creator helps us become more than we thought we could be. Before we hung up, Captain James told me, "I will count this as the third great reason why I'm still alive. You can count on my loyalty; I will send you all of the documents you've requested. They will be in your e-mail in the morning."

He paused for a moment, as if gathering his thoughts, and then said, "How did you know to ask me?" I replied that one of my mentors opened my eyes to who he was. "And what is that?" James asked.

"A successful master ship captain, blessed with undaunted courage and strength," I said.

"I'm glad you think so highly of me!" James replied, with delight.

The next morning, true to his word, an impeccable resume brief and a comprehensive CV arrived via email along with a list of accommodations, professional references, and his insight on the ship requirements for a successful voyage. James also sent recommendations for first and second mates.

I had to stay focused on my current commitments, despite how excited I was getting about this new venture. I was still burning the candle at both ends. I was learning how to make the time that I had more productive, as well as more prosperous. For the first time in my career, I was specifically delegating tasks both in my current career and my new one. I was in the thick of it and truly learning the gifts and skills of entrepreneurship. I was also gaining a great deal of respect for those brave souls who had ventured before me. Things were moving along in both areas, and for the most part, I felt very edified. But I was torn by the fact that my heart and passion were focused on the sea and I needed to take time to enjoy the moment, as well as prepare for the journey that was becoming reality.

Dwight had gone over all the documents for the company with me. I was nominated as the president; the vice president was Stephen, a retired accountant who was willing to step up to the plate with a capital investment. He was a true team player who had a philanthropic interest in the expedition. He'd worked in public and private company firms and had amassed a deep network of clients and friends who expressed a serious interest in participating in the expedition, either through contributions or personal service. It was very apparent that Stephen had done very well, both personally and professionally. He often said, "successful people have successful ways."

Clayton was selected as an advisory member to help increase the probability of success as he was the only team member who had prior experience with the expedition area. He was willing to contribute however he could. He was in this adventure for love and passion.

The rest of the board members were selected for their skills and experience. All of them would have to work together for the common good and all of them would help direct, guide, protect, and grow the company. They would need to make righteous decisions pertaining to corporate governance and direction. It was decided that there would be a total of five directors, each with a specific set of skills and talents in his or her own field.

Candace had been in business for herself for more than a few different companies and professional fields, she had many gifts, skills, and talents. She had the ability to overcome and worked well with others and had risen to the top of her field.

The next director whom we selected without hesitation was Emma. She was wise beyond her years which was evident from a single meeting. She also owned her own business and had risen from a seven-plus year illness. She was a miracle and the more I learned about her, the more convinced I became that she was a complex problem solver and was very strong and spirited. Although very gifted and highly skilled, she was also extremely humble. She made sure we all knew she could hold her own and not to mistake her meekness for weakness.

The third director was Ashley, also a leader both personally and professionally. She had a reputation for courage and strength and being able to see the good in even the darkest of times. She was also very talented and believed that we learn forever. She was a tough lady and a loving mother who did well in all things.

The next board member was Jim, a well-educated capitalist who was very familiar with all types of companies and financial markets. He had built a thirty-year financial base and network and had walked away from another company because he was unwilling to compromise his integrity. He would also act as interim chairman of the board until my safe return from sea.

The final board member was David. He had learned from adversity and had faced many goliaths in his life. He had been to the school of life as well as formally educated by some great mentors and had risen through the corporate ranks and served on the boards of both startup companies and well-established businesses, and had also built a powerful network who championed his causes and provided capital and service.

As the organization came together, I realized it was time to choose a name for it. Although we thought of many, eventually we selected "A Legacy of Treasure." The name was approved and the company was suddenly very real. Thoughts of abundance, prosperity, and wealth once again came to mind.

I was in constant communication with the captain; James said that he'd selected Andrew as his first mate and Peter as the second mate. He also introduced me to Matthew and Simon who were highly skilled on the seas and part of his elite crew. Their CVs and resumes, references, and other documents had already been sent along as well as a broker auction and wholesale inventory list of ships that were available. I had heard of auctions and bank direct sales but had never participated in one. James suggested that it might be worth our time to go to one. All of this happened in just a few weeks.

I picked up the phone to schedule another meeting with Edwin. His secretary put me on hold for a few minutes, and then asked if I could meet in a couple of hours.

"Yes," I responded, surprised that he could see me so soon. It took a few minutes to rearrange my work schedule, but I found a way to make it work. I grabbed my tablet and other documents, and headed to Edwin's office. As I pulled the old Volvo into Edwin's office parking lot, I took a moment to mediate and find a prayer. I grabbed my backpack, and opened the car door. As soon as I stood up, the words of my friend entered my mind: "the noble ones." I opened the office door.

When I arrived, the receptionist greeted me with a warm smile and said, "Christian, follow me." She led the way to a very nice conference room. She indicated that I be seated in a large leather chair at the side of the table. I sat down and she quietly closed the door; I was the only one in the room.

At the front of the room was a large, blank whiteboard. Off to the right was a detailed timeline with dates, pictures, and market areas as well as pictures of very nice places and what looked to be artifacts. I studied it briefly and saw that it was a visual history of Edwin's company. It was like a comprehensive look into the chronological success of my friend and mentor. This was truly the most incredible overview of success I had seen.

The door opened and Edwin entered, wasting no time. He said, "I believe that if you can see it, you can build it. Some people told me that this company was only a dream, but I saw it in my mind and I felt it in my heart. Then, with a lot of faith and passion, I pursued some of my life's work. Christian, I know you have a Gantt chart but it's time to put your dreams further into visual form with a realistic timeline. Look at it daily, and let it take root and percolate into your subconscious. You combine that with the great, gifted, skilled, and talented people focused and moving in the right direction and add continued action and a lot of faith, and it will work for you. Christian, think of it like this: if you have a small fishing vessel and all the fisherman start moving the oars in different directions, you will either move in circles or tread your position and not progress at all. However, if all the fisherman row in the same direction, your vessel will begin to head where you want to go. I believe this will work for you as it has for me."

With that, Edwin took a seat close to the conference room door.

I had become accustomed to his office and sitting across from him. Nevertheless, the company was growing and change was inevitable.

"Dwight has updated me on your progress," he said. "You have done well." He looked at his watch. "One moment," he said. He got up, opened the conference room door, walked out, and returned with Captain James followed by a woman I didn't know. "I received the same e-mails you did, and my secretary booked him a ticket just after you spoke to the captain," Edwin explained. "We were hoping to help speed up the process. So, let's all get acquainted and get down to business." Edwin smiled, closed the conference room door, and turned to the woman.

"This is Phoebe," he said, "I was introduced to her through Paul, an incredible leader and mentor. She has also been very successful in many areas of her life. She's well-seasoned in successful business plan modeling and forecasting, I think she'll be a valuable asset to have going forward."

Phoebe moved around the table shaking hands and smiling. "I'm happy to be here," she said, "This is an exciting venture."

"We're thrilled to have someone with your expertise on board," I said, shaking her hand.

She took a seat across the table from me and set down a tablet in front of her. "Edwin has asked me to compile all of the data we discuss and use it to create a ten-year business model with a one-hundred-year overview. That way, the corporate teams and potential investors or shareholders can also get a picture of where the company is planning on going and set realistic expectations. And if we're successful," she said looking pointedly at Captain James, "then those relevant parties will be able to identify the risks and the possible upside as well as the possible legacy that could make history."

"She will also help identify the strengths, weaknesses, opportunities, threats, and other pertinent market cycles and trends," Edwin said. "We're very lucky to have her on board."

"That sounds great," I said.

Edwin nodded and grabbed a marker. On the left-hand side of the whiteboard, he wrote the new corporate structure. Then off to the right, he put the team structure. James, his first mate, Andrew, and second mate, Peter. The captain listed all of the shipmates and their positions. Then, he said, the time had come to decide on the capital needed and to choose a ship. He drew an arrow from the corporate side pointing inward, then an arrow from James's side also pointing inward. Then he drew the outline of a nice-sized ship. He looked up and pointed to the ship and said, "There are many ships that will take us to our dreams."

James and I both nodded in agreement.

Edwin continued, "James, of the three ships you've inspected and reviewed, which would be your last choice?" James told him and Edwin noted it on the board. "Now," Edwin asked, "What is your first choice?" James told him that as well. "Okay," Edwin said, making note of the remaining ship on the board. "Since this one is the one in the middle, what don't you like about it?"

"It's actually the best for design and engine strength," James replied. "But the majority of all the communication and navigation and tracking equipment would need to either be updated or replaced."

"All right, as for the first choice, let's talk about this one," Edwin said.

"Even though it's a smaller ship with less engine capacity, we can make it work," James said. "The technology is up to date, but the price is high compared to the other two."

"James," asked Edwin, "What do you think it would cost to have the larger vessel retrofitted and updated?"

Without hesitation, James replied, "Within our budget, but we'll have to allow for a little overage."

"How long would it take?" Edwin asked.

"We would need to get the updating and retrofitting bid out and the work scheduled to know for sure," Captain James said. "I had a good look at this ship and with all the current technology, I have never seen a deck prism on a ship of this magnitude and certainly not on any ship for many, many years. This had to be a custom build by someone who had a love of history and knew that a deck prism or deck light could provide light from natural sources. This may prove invaluable."

Edwin was excited. He looked at me and said, "I believe we should take the larger ship with a more powerful engine."

"How did you arrive at that decision?" I asked.

He smiled. "First, remember that I asked you to think in terms of abundance, prosperity, and wealth?"

"Yes," I replied.

"I believe in you," he said, "I believe in the captain, and I believe it was a higher source that brought us all here today. I also believe in myself as I would hope, Christian, you will always believe in yourself. Second, the weight of your newfound treasure can sometimes be overwhelming, not only in terms of the physical weight, but also mentally. You will need this ship for the added team weight. You will need to surround yourself with the right individuals so that you can handle every aspect. That means you'll have to select the right crew based on expertise, gifts, and proven talent as well as finding possible mentors on the business and corporate side. By doing this as James did with Andrew and Peter, and you have recently demonstrated with the choices you've made regarding your corporate board officers, you increase your chances for success. In other words, if you put the right people in the right places, your chances for a successful venture typically increase."

Throughout this discussion, I noticed that Phoebe was taking detailed notes and condensing everything we discussed.

Edwin capped the marker he'd been gesturing with and set it down on the table.

"Now," he continued, "back to the third reason; the larger ship is right for this voyage. After the retrofitting and updating, it will have the most up-to-date equipment and cutting-edge technology available for the open seas, not to mention with the current softness of the large ship market, we stand to save a great deal. In the end, with a purchase well below market value, we could save a few million dollars. To my mind, that's a million dollars earned. So here's what I think; if you and James let me know the estimated time to get to your destinations and provide me with a timeline and written expense estimations, I can set an updated budget and expense investment level that I'm comfortable with. The ship is the most expensive investment, and I will hold the ownership to that with an agreement that you can handle. In the event that your search does not bear fruit, I will have something of value to recuperate some or all of my investment; the larger ships with the updated equipment and state of the art technology. With a market rebound, the demand for this type of vessel will surely increase. You should explore that with your newly-formed board and attorney. I feel Stephen will be a great asset in these decisions as well. Now that your ship has been selected, you might want to consider some other angels or benefactors. I would do this after you know what your updated budget will be. When I started my company, I underestimated my expenses, and this caused delays and setbacks, not to mention a great deal of stress."

Edwin pulled a chair from the table and sat down. He smiled at us both. "As I grew in business and consulted with seasoned professionals, they advised me to overestimate when I needed to capitalize and to start a reserve fund. That way when the economy changed, we could weather the storm. And if I only used what I had to, I could typically negotiate other areas to keep my cost reasonable." Edwin turned to address James directly, "Captain James, you have guts; you came here without discussing a firm fee arrangement. Might I ask what you're thinking?"

James smiled, indicating that he'd made it a practice early in his personal and professional life to fully understand the professional mission or stewardship as well as what and who would be involved before entering into a contract of obligation. "I made this a habit in my personal life and felt the practice had benefited those I chose to do business with. Now that I more fully understand the expedition, those currently involved, the trade routes, and the voyage," James paused for a moment, moved closer to Edwin and myself, smiled, and said, "I would estimate this type of expedition would take between 40 and 70 days. Keep in mind, this timeline has some unknown variables such as ocean conditions, weather, and what we discover. That being said, I would do it for the love of the sea and a small percentage of the find. Here's what I was thinking."

James looked down at his tablet, took his pen, and wrote a number on it and then passed it to Edwin. I looked at it for a brief moment and noted that the majority of the compensation was based upon the success of the expedition. It was the first time I had seen Edwin beam. "Ingenious!" he said. "James, you never cease to amaze me."

James looked at both Edwin and myself and said, "Please put the NDAs in place and the contracts for the crew before mine. And if you could have Human Resources take care of the family documents as well, that will ease my mind and I can shift my focus on retrofitting and updating the ship. It can possibly help save some time as well and help Christian find the final shipmates."

James, reiterated, "Please take care of all the other ship hands, mates, and their families before me."

Edwin looked over at me. "Well, Christian?" he said.

I looked at Captain James and smiled. "Captain, you were kind enough to keep me in the loop on contract negotiations and send over the emails on each of the current crew members. All the contracts are ready for each of your mates. I will have yours sent for your review first thing in the morning."

James smiled. "The joy is in the journey," he said.

I looked at Edwin and he smiled, "What do you think?" he asked.

I said, "Captain James, your percent of such a find would be an incredible amount."

"Yes," the captain replied. "Christian, if we are blessed with such a find, give some thought to all the people who go hungry each day. I believe if we find even a portion of what you seek, it could be life altering and do a lot of good for so many in a multitude of ways."

"Christian, let's work with Dwight and get the offer prepared for the purchase of the ship the Captain recommends. James gave us a starting place and an all cash offer should get their attention. I have learned over the years that financial institutions unfortunately pre-plan for annual losses and this may provide an opportunity for a willing buyer and a willing seller to strike a deal."

James nodded in agreement, and said, "You have your captain, the captain has a crew, and we will soon have our ship ready for the open seas. Edwin and Christian, make no mistake about it: this is one of the reasons I am still here." The room filled with silence that felt spiritual in nature.

Edwin looked over at Phoebe and asked her to stay and visit for a few minutes. He then turned to Captain James and I and said, "Gentlemen, this time has been well spent." Edwin stood and gave each of us a signature hug and said, "There is great work to be done here and it is with great anticipation that I look forward to our next meeting. Be at peace."

Persistence will provide the keys that unlock the doors to abundant resources.

9. FOR EVERYONE
THAT ASKETH

I WAS AWOKEN BY A WARM LICK TO MY FACE. I GOT MY BEARINGS AND looked at the clock. I realized that in her excitement to go for a walk, Sadie had woken me up before sunrise. I think she must have been taking the old quote, "Early to bed and early to rise will make one healthy, wealthy, and wise" very seriously.

As I looked into Sadie's big, golden eyes, I could see going back to sleep wasn't in the cards. Sadie had been patient with me as I balanced my newfound business venture with my career and busy work schedule. I owed her this much at least.

We both grabbed a light snack and headed out to one of Sadie's favorite trails. She liked the trail by the local park, as it led to a grove of trees and an incredible view. Sadie enjoyed the walk. On the trail there was a small pond with a few birds whom she loved to run after. The birds always eluded her, but she enjoyed the chase.

A few minutes later, Sadie was back by my side and we headed down the trail together. I glanced at my watch and saw that I still had plenty of time to get ready for my day. I was glad to be on Sadie's schedule for once, as the past few weeks had flown by. She must have known that I needed a quiet, early morning with her.

We arrived at the house, both better for the time we'd spent together. I had gotten into the habit of meditating, praying, and reading a few pages out of an incredible book before going into work. This habit allowed me to feed my mind and soul and combined with the time I'd spent with Sadie on the trail, I was reinvigorated and ready for the day.

When I arrived at my office, I saw that there was plenty to do and limited time in which to do it. When I finally returned all my calls, it was late afternoon. I only had a short window of time before I was expected at Edwin's office. I wrapped up a few more things and headed out. As the elevator doors began to close, a hand reached out and stopped them. In stepped Linda, the current president of the firm from which I was getting ready to resign. She smiled at me.

"Christian," she said, "there is a lot going on right now and I appreciate your commitment and focus. Life can throw a lot at us sometimes." I just smiled in response. "I hope you're headed some place where you can get some rest," she continued.

"Sort of," I said. "And you?"

"I'm headed to a genealogy class," she said. "Have a great evening."

"You too," I said as the elevator doors opened. I waved goodbye to her and headed to my Volvo.

When I pulled into Edwin's office parking lot prior to my meeting with Edwin and some of the exploration team members, I took a few minutes to meditate and visualize what I hoped to accomplish.

Upon entering, I received the customary professional greeting and was led to a familiar conference room. I sat down next to Captain James and we spoke briefly before Edwin joined us. As he came through the door, I noticed that he seemed especially jubilant. He greeted us both. "Gentlemen," he said, "remind me why you are both here today."

"You know my love of the sea," James said. "And the opportunity to be with such an elite crew and part of the exploration voyage we are about to embark on is part of my life's mission. It's a dream come true," he said.

Edwin smiled and replied, "Captain, do you believe there are many vessels that will ignite our passions and allow for us to fulfill our dreams and purpose?"

"Absolutely," James answered. "My life is a living testimony to the truth of that and so much more."

"Thank you, James," Edwin said. "Christian? Any thoughts?"

"If I understand correctly," I said, "every individual has an infinite worth and purpose. We may travel many different paths and implement an array of systems and values to accomplish this work.

We will encounter heartache, loss, and setbacks. There are times we may feel we are in the deep valleys of the Himalayas, but we must remember that seasons change. As we grow and learn, we should be ever mindful of the blessings and joy in the journey."

Edwin replied, "Christian, you are starting to see with your heart. There is great inner strength in this and with focused action and the right help, you can accomplish all that you were put here to do."

Edwin then turned to Captain James and asked how things were going with the crew.

"Edwin," James said, "we should have at least twelve crew members for whom we are working to complete contracts, as well as Jared, a multi-lingual, well-seasoned shipbuilder who also worked as an elite shipmate."

"Jared is a friend of mine," I explained. "He speaks English, Spanish, Hebrew, K'iche, a Mayan language spoken in Guatemala, and Mixe-Zoquean, more common to parts of Mexico," I said.

"He sounds like he'd be very useful indeed," Edwin commented.

"He will be," I said. "And I trust him implicitly." I looked at the list on the board for a moment then asked, "Do we need a medic? Someone who can handle any medical emergencies that might occur?"

Captain James spoke up. "I believe my friend Nathanial would be happy to join us," he said. "He is a doctor and has worked on several of my previous voyages. We'd been looking for an opportunity to set out together on the open seas again." At that, his lips curled into a smile.

"Excellent," Edwin said. "That's settled then."

"If I may," Captain James continued, "Simon, a former shipmate of mine is someone with whom I have undertaken several voyages. I think he could also be of use."

"What is his specialty?" Edwin asked.

Captain James smiled and replied, "Simon has been upon some of the roughest Northern waters imaginable. He is an elite shipmate, well-skilled in all forms of navigation. He could take a ship through the darkest of nights and stay the correct course. Growing up, he spent a good portion of his youth on the open seas and he has owned his own commercial fishing vessel before. He is one of the few individuals I know that can still use a sextant. He is one of the most courageous people we could have with us on this voyage. In each of the shipmates' eyes – as in Simon's – you will see a certain zeal. Like the rest of the crew, he is ready."

"If he comes with your recommendation, it sounds like he will be an excellent addition," Edwin said. "Christian?"

"Sounds great to me," I said. "I think we'd be lucky to have him."

The captain nodded, pleased.

"So that brings the total number of people to fifteen, excluding myself," I said. Edwin and Captain James nodded in agreement.

Edwin said that he had reviewed the pedigrees of all of the ship mates and had discovered that they were all very gifted and highly skilled individuals who could handle the ship in the event of an emergency. "How did you find them so quickly?" he asked Captain James.

"I consulted with a higher power," the captain replied.

"Well done!" said Edwin. "Let's talk about the crew members we still need. Over the past twenty-five years or so, I've learned a lot about why many of my competitors have come and gone. Successful people have successful ways. They know how to surround themselves with gifts, specific knowledge, or talents, and the right amount of energy for success. Looking back, I would recommend that you seek individuals who will help you with your larger mission of bringing about change for the better. Search for people who hold the long view."

Edwin stood up, walked to the whiteboard, and said, "Phoebe and I have all the information for the crew in the business and corporate formation files." With that, he erased the board and wrote the word "gifts" in large, bold letters. Then he turned to Captain James and said, "I respect your years of experience. Feel free to interject at any time. Christian, let's discuss the word 'gifts' as there are many. Some are temporal and some are spiritual and I would like to hear from your perspective what gifts you believe the individuals you have selected for your company possess."

"James, I respect your years of experience and past success," he said, "which is why I'm looking at my friend and president of this voyage and asking him, 'At this point of the journey, what are you thinking?'"

"Honesty," I said automatically.

"Yes," Edwin replied. "That would be on the top of my list."

"And integrity," I added.

"Yes, if you build anything without having either of these, you are building on sand. It won't last," Edwin concurred.

"The third," I replied, "is faith."

Why faith?" he asked.

"Faith is the hope in things not seen, but rather those to come," I explained. "That certainly seems fitting for this kind of expedition."

"Yes," Edwin agreed.

"I believe if you surround yourself in the power of belief, all things become possible," I said. "And the fifth is desire. If you truly have desire, it motivates you in the direction of your dreams."

"You have been listening," Edwin smiled. "May I share a little food for thought, Christian?"

"Sure," I replied, "I appreciate learning from you."

Edwin chuckled and said, "Try to remember – as I have learned over the years – that wisdom is knowledge rightly applied."

"I will," I said.

"So true," Captain James said.

"The sixth," he continued, "is having the right individuals in the right place producing the right results for the right reasons. The seventh is love," he said, writing it down. "This is one of the greatest powers on Earth. If one truly loves what one does, it is manifested in all that they do. Love is the key ingredient that binds all the other attributes, gifts, and talents together."

He turned back to the board to continue writing. "The eighth is passion about life and all it has to offer. A truly passionate indi-vidual has a deep desire and dream to live their best life as they are forever learning. The ninth is unity. Mavericks are great in the business world, but no one is an island unto themselves. It can get lonely at the top and there is great strength in unity. The tenth is vision—you want the individuals you surround yourself with to be able to moderately envision your direction, goals, and dreams. A picture is worth a thousand words but even a small glimpse into eternity has had a lasting impact on many individuals."

I found myself nodding along and sneaking glances at Captain James who sat, watching and listening.

"The eleventh is worth," Edwin continued. "When an individual realizes that they are of infinite worth and they can say, 'I will add value to who I meet and what I do,' confidence will radiate. The last is charity. I have met people over the years who believed charity starts at home. This is only a small part of what charity is; there are countless examples of charity if we look around us. It is one of the most powerful gifts we possess. It can motivate us to become more than we ever thought possible. I know what it's like to receive charity as well as give it. If your heart is in the right place, I can tell you that a wealth of blessings will follow, but you must take action in all of these," he said, pointing to the list on the whiteboard.

I looked over at Captain James; his face a wrinkled map of the storms and trials he had seen. His wise eyes had watered, but he looked straight ahead. Then Edwin said, "Hire as you were planning to, while asking what they can add to your crew. Go forward with faith. We don't have much time. Captain James, secure the ship purchase." "President," he said with a smile, looking at me, "work with the captain and his mates, fill the positions, and we will meet as soon as you are finished and ready to discuss the embarkment of the voyage."

James stood up and shook Edwin's hand. "I greatly appreciate the time as well as the opportunity." He turned to me, smiled, and said, "We have great work to do. I will be in touch shortly." I nodded and he turned and left.

Edwin closed the door, sat down, and said, "What are you going to do about your current career? You will set sail in a new direction; do you have it worked out?" I replied that I had worked over the past couple of months to delegate a lot of my workload and that it was looking increasingly like I'd be given the opportunity for a graceful exit, given the impending merger. "What had first seemed like a problem now looks like an opportunity," I said.

"I'm glad to hear it," Edwin said.

"I'm ahead of schedule now," I explained. "At first, I was only going to take a couple of months off, but now I realize this wouldn't be possible. "Out of fairness to the company that has treated me well, I have drafted a formal resignation and plan to turn it in next week. This will give them 30 days' notice."

"That is very wise," Edwin said. "There are times when you need both your current position as well as the dream. In your situation, you need to move forward quickly. You've just shown me, one of your financial benefactors, that you believe enough in your ability to succeed that by letting go of the sure thing, you have demonstrated your faith in what is to come. Well done."

I asked, "Out of all of the gifts for success, what are your top two or three?"

Edwin smiled. "It is simple," he said. "Faith. It has been said that faith can move mountains. This has been true throughout both my business failures and successes. I have had faith in divinity, a higher power, and a purpose other than myself. Over time, you come to know that you are not alone. Every good and righteous endeavor brings with it the help of great and noble ones and forces beyond our understanding. But, make no mistake, in any great success, I have had divine help; even if it was merely a prompting or a small inner voice. Yes, I have witnessed miracles, but those are sacred. When one puts one's faith in divine help, greatness happens. Captain James said that he prayed and many things became possible for him." Edwin looked me in the eyes with his soul-piercing look that I had come to know well and said, "Christian, as you increase in abundance and wealth, remember that money is just a tool like any other tool in your toolbox. It can be used for good or evil."

Tears came to my eyes as I reflected on what the captain and my oyster had said. They had both mentioned "a great and noble purpose."

"For me," Edwin continued, "The second is belief, because the energy that you send out when you truly believe is distributed throughout the universe. It is felt by everyone with whom you come into contact. Belief has taken the very destitute and poor to heights previously unimagined. You must believe in yourself if others are ever going to believe in you."

"I am learning," I said. "Belief and a leap of faith go hand in hand."

Edwin nodded. "And finally," he said, "you must believe in what you are doing. Belief keeps the naysayers at bay."

He looked at me carefully. "You asked for three," he said. "Charity would be the third. Every great, successful individual I have met had a higher purpose for their wealth. Some were on such a large scale that it took their whole being to sustain it. Others were manageable. This is also part of the reason that I believe those who have wealth were allowed the privilege of it. I have never heard about anyone regretting charity. Some of the most charitable people in history were the great ancient and noble ones and they made tremendous sacrifices."

I looked up. There was that phrase again.

Edwin continued, "Then there are people just like you who found their higher purpose as their dreams unfolded. There were many business owners who helped individuals and families gain their freedom and safety during horrific war times. At the end of those times, even though they had helped thousands, they all wished they could have done more. They truly found and came to know themselves while in the service of others."

"I understand," I said as I continued to think about the greater purpose for our individual journeys.

Edwin continued, "All situations are different, but believe me, charity will bring wisdom into your life. There is, of course, another aspect to charity; the giving of yourself, your talents, and your gifts. Charity does not always involve financial gifts. Think of it as mentoring. One of the real reasons I got involved in your business venture was to mentor you. Then you, in turn, will be able to share this wisdom with someone else. As you become successful, more opportunities for mentoring will present themselves. This way, the parable of the talents will live on."

"I am very grateful for your mentorship," I said.

Edwin nodded. "Years ago," he said, "I began to give a percentage of my earnings to my faith and the deity that I believe in. Their funds also serve a higher purpose. Mathematically, it doesn't make sense, but I have found that I cannot out-give the deity. I have received many blessings in my life due to this one simple commitment. You will have to decide for yourself, but I believe it is one of the greatest strengths and reasons for my success." Edwin paused and smiled at me. "Christian, I am sure James would agree with me on this: when I was a young man, I wanted things to go much faster than they sometimes did. But looking back over the years, the love and joy was found in the journey. Christian, I will update Phoebe on our progress so she is not held up. I appreciate meeting with you." With that, Edwin stood up, walked me out, gave me a familiar handshake, and wished me a great evening.

I looked back to see the Captain standing in the parking lot, looking up into the sky. I climbed into my car and pulled up beside him. "Is everything all right?" I asked.

"Never better, Christian," he said. "I was taking a moment to enjoy the beauty of the Master's hand when a mesmerizing bluish white shooting star traveled across this deep blue sky. I was reflecting on Edwin and the loss he suffered when he lost Levi at such a young age. I would surmise that those who are here only a short while are like that shooting star. They share their light with us for a short time but their brightness and light travels where it is most needed. Then there are people like me," he gestured to himself. "I have lived a long life. Like the old stars that show up each night, I keep going. Possibly before my journey's end, I may be filled with enough light to brighten a dark night." He turned away from the sky, looked me in the eyes, and smiled a warm smile. "With that, Christian," he said, "I am heading home."

"Good night, Captain," I said.

"You as well," he replied.

By faith and the required action, what was once a dream has now become reality.

10. RECEIVETH

NEVER LET THE FEAR OF STRIKING OUT KEEP YOU FROM PLAYING THE game. I found myself having some very human moments like we all do; occasionally a negative thought or brief moment of doubt would pass through my mind. In those times, I found self-talk, prayer, and meditation to be useful tools for helping me to maintain my focus on the path to success. I would also listen to inspirational music and audiobooks. I had been told by a professor once that if we did not choose to feed our mind, someone else would feed it for us. That said, I found some of the most mind clearing and inspirational moments to be walks with Sadie in the cool sand next to the sounds of the breaking, salty ocean waves; that always seem to speak to my heart and soul.

Captain James was a true leader; he was very focused and task-driven. We assisted Michelle, the new VP of Human Resources, as she made sure each shipmate, team member, and their families were provided with a quality benefit package including disability and health insurance. We wanted the team members and their families to know we valued each of them and worked to ensure they had some sense of peace while their loved ones were away at sea. It was interesting for me to learn how many people only wanted to be involved if financial security was guaranteed beyond this voyage. We were honest and forthright with everyone who applied and it paid dividends. We let those interested individuals know that this mission might be a one-time thing, or it might result in many more voyages to follow. The calculated risk was greater than a normal career path or business venture, but the potential rewards were very high and though there were many people to choose from, only a few were called.

I submitted my formal resignation to Ronnie, the Vice President, and my current boss. We mutually agreed that I would stay on for the next thirty days and do what I could to prepare the company for the merger, which was no longer a rumor but had become reality. When I was in the office one day, I was asked to meet with Linda, the president, and Ronnie. Anticipating the meeting, my heart began to pound.

Upon arriving at the executive conference room, I was greeted by Linda and Ronnie; they asked me to sit and asked about my future plans. Since I was no longer going to be part of the company to which I had given long hours and dedicated work, they were naturally curious about my next steps.

I looked up at Linda and Ronnie and said, "I first want to let you know that I have appreciated working here. You took a chance on me and I tried to exceed your expectations. Now, I feel I need to take a chance on myself and believe in fulfilling some of my life's work and answer an inner calling."

After a moment, Ronnie looked at me and said, "You were next in line for a promotion." Then he wrote something on a slip of paper and slid it over to me. "That would be your new bonus and annual salary package plus a few perks," he said.

I was surprised; it was a large number. I thanked him and pushed the paper back towards him.

Ronnie took it and looked down at it. "What would it take to keep you on?" he asked.

"While I appreciate your position and this generous proposal," I said, "I have to believe, have faith, and take the right course of action for some of my life's work."

They both looked at me with bewilderment. "So you'll be joining one of our competitors?" Linda asked.

"No," I replied. I took a deep breath and explained. "Ever since I was a young child, I have wanted to set out on the ocean in search of artifacts and treasures. As you both know, my education is in ancient history and business. The doors of opportunity have opened to make this dream possible. The initial trip could take two to three months, depending on weather conditions, and I feel that it isn't right to take the time off from this company with the intention of returning when my heart would be elsewhere."

Linda nodded, though I could tell she was surprised. "That's admirable of you," she said.

I had learned a fair amount about Linda over the years I'd been with the company. She had lost her husband in the prime of their lives to an accident and had risen out of the darkness to spiritual and financial success. She was forever being included in lists of powerful women – where she rightly belonged – but she was much more complex than those lists would lead one to believe. Her favorite hobby was genealogy. She loved bringing families and loved ones together. I respected her greatly and felt that her wishes for my success were genuine.

They both wished me success and said they would be in touch.

"I appreciate the way you've conducted yourself," the president spoke up. "You've made this as seamless as possible considering the transitions we're facing."

"The company has been good to me," I said. "It's the least I can do."

Although it had been intense, it was a necessary meeting.

As the week went on, I was able to wrap up the loose ends at the office and pass the torch to my successor as well as help Captain James prepare for our next meeting.

Toward the end of my first week after giving notice, I was invited into Linda's office unexpectedly.

"I have given some thought to what you are about to do," she said after I sat down. "We would like this company to be one of your sponsors. Should you be as successful as you've been here, the company would benefit."

"That's incredibly generous," I said.

"There is the historical value to consider as well," she added. "We would spend the funds on marketing anyway."

I asked if it would be all right if I got back to her the following week. This was incredible. Edwin was right; abundance, prosperity, and wealth *do* come when that is where your thoughts and actions reside.

I was enthralled as I watched Captain James and our shipmates, Andrew and Peter meet and interview additional, highly-skilled crew members. They would be an incredible asset to any voyage, and they also knew the old ways of navigating by the stars, the heavens, and other celestial markers. Captain James shook each of their hands in turn and welcomed them aboard. "Celestial navigation should never be understated or undervalued. You and Edwin have been speaking about it and it never hurts to have those with you who have a strong sense of direction."

Captain James looked over me, "Christian," he asked, "Do you know what a sextant is?"

"Captain, if I remember correctly," I said, "it's an instrument used to determine the angle between the horizon and either the sun, moon, or a star to determine longitude and latitude."

Captain James replied, "That will do for now," and smiled.

I received a call from Aaliyah. "Edwin asked that I call you and let you know the offer on the ship has been accepted," she said. She told me the ship was being sent over to the proper dock so the updating and retrofitting could be taken care of.

We found our spirits quite elevated by the news that the ship we'd chosen could be ready ahead of schedule. There'd been a cancellation and the retrofitting and updating would be completed earlier than anticipated, allowing us to cast off ahead of schedule. I can contribute a large part of that milestone to the wisdom of Edwin and Captain James and a well-qualified firm doing the work right down to the last detail including the installation of the satellite boosters and an additional fuel tank. I was elated to be in the company of so many professional and qualified individuals. Captain James let everyone know the expedition would soon be upon us.

We had also received more good news; the estimated seven to ten weeks for this type of retrofitting could be done in three to four weeks, including the additional communications equipment and safety items required by Captain James. The captain said that we could begin our ocean voyage ahead of schedule.

After consulting with Edwin, I notified Linda, the president and CEO of the company I still worked for, that we would accept her capital and sponsorship offer. Linda's attorney and our corporate attorney, Dwight, worked to finalize a registered offering that would let her invest her capital and become a sponsor. I was grateful to have a seasoned professional who was familiar with what was required to keep the company on the right path and ensure our compliance with the capital and fundraising markets. He indicated we could also raise a limited amount from other possible investors and sponsors as long as they met the requirements and read and signed the proper documents. The transaction closed in less than ten days. Edwin had learned over the years that when an opportunity like that is forthcoming, you make it happen. He shared with me that a majority of the time, the difference between failure and success is being prepared.

The weekend arrived and both the captain and I decided to come up for air. He would set his affairs in order with his family and I would do the same. We would regroup on Monday and meet with Edwin that following Tuesday.

After wrapping up loose ends at the office, I headed home to grab Sadie for a sunset walk along the shoreline, the waves cresting in the distance. After about an hour, my mind was clear and I walked up the beach, found a quiet spot, sat down, and just listened. The sound of the waves came over me and I thought about what Edwin and Captain James had spoken about: divinity and prayer. I decided to meditate. I visualized the actual ship and expedition in my mind, along with a trove of artifacts and treasures untold; the return and success of the overall journey. I also thought about a higher purpose and the individuals I could help. It was as clear as the setting sun. It was beautiful. I was truly in the present moment. I stood up but I felt like I wasn't finished. I sat back down; I couldn't get Captain James' words out of my mind. I prayed and kept it simple and full of gratitude for what I had learned and the doors that had been opened for my own understanding and wisdom. I sat for a moment longer.

The rays of the sun bathed my face with a warm zeal, and the waves of the ocean spoke to my heart and soul.

Listening to the cresting waves and a moment of prayer and meditation combined with the warmth of the dissipating rays of the sun, I felt a peaceful warmth touch my body and soul. It was time to head home and put things in order for the coming months. Fortunately for me, Sadie would join the crew and make the journey with us; I needed her as my own first mate.

I was rested when Monday morning came and after I arrived at the office, things moved along quickly. I found I was counting down the days until we departed. Captain James and I agreed to meet that afternoon. We went over the decisions we'd made and the crew we'd selected.

"Christian," he asked, "have you noticed each of the selected crew members have some common gifts?"

"Yes," I replied.

"Would you share some of those with me?" he asked.

I responded that each crew member had the ability to lead, but was humble enough to serve in whatever position they were recruited for.

"Go on," James said.

"I noticed that each of them has a distinctive personality, different from everyone else, but all are pioneers in their field and from some of their experiences, they have demonstrated great faith and a true ability to discern. This was apparent in some of the choices they've made."

"Keep going," he said.

"Let me think for a moment," I said, taking a second to pause and reflect. "All right, each of them had different strengths than the others, but as a crew, they all seem to integrate somehow. They compensate for each other's weaknesses and become stronger together." Then I remembered what I'd read about how they had all continued to learn and how they all enjoyed teaching. "Captain James," I said, "there was something special I noticed as well. Each of them had a personal experience witnessing the great and noble ones. All of them have a sense of a higher purpose."

The Captain nodded, smiling slightly.

"I'm sure I've only touched on some of their gifts," I said. "But I'll end with this: I can already tell that each of them has already learned that knowledge is wisdom rightly applied." I smiled. "And," I said, "I was relieved to learn that some of them come from humble beginnings and each of them asked me what I thought of fishing. A few indicated that when this voyage was over, I would be able to navigate a vessel and know how to fish."

He smiled. "What else have you noticed?" he asked.

"Each of them had the courage and motivation to set out upon the open sea," I said.

The captain agreed with me and said, "Yes, they are all focused on a common goal. I have found over the years that when you have focus and unity working in harmony, your destination is reached much more quickly. Also having harmony, unity, and courage can help you through even the worst of times. There was another gift that each of them possessed, some in much greater degrees than others, but all of them had it in some form. It can get interesting out on the open and rough seas. Humor can sometimes carry you even in the worst of times; it can make a situation bearable. When I was ill, I learned that prayer, faith, laughter and meditation, combined with the fasting and prayers of others and true friendship were some of the greatest gifts I could ever be blessed with."

I had never been in a situation of survival, but I felt the spirit of what Captain James spoke about. I also respected the captain and wanted to heed his words.

We parted for the evening with confidence in ourselves and the crew. The next day would be a day of faith and action, and Captain James's words of prayer, faith, and the prayers of others sunk deep into my soul. I had been well-mentored and fed in a multitude of ways.

As I returned home, I could see Sadie's golden eyes and smiling face in the window. We could both use a walk. The morning would be upon me soon, so after we returned from our walk, I took a few minutes for meditation and prayer, two very real tools for progress and success.

You are the creator of your own masterpiece;
it's time to pick up your brush
and make your art.

11. AND THEY THAT ASKETH

Upon entering the reception area of Edwin's office, I was greeted by Aaliyah, his senior assistant. She let me know that it would be a few minutes before Edwin was ready for me and that I should take a seat. I had gotten to know Aaliyah over the past few years. She had been Edwin's assistant for several years; before that, she was a paralegal working for Edwin's company. She was very gifted and eminently professional and well versed in both the corporate and humanitarian worlds, making her an ideal person to work for Edwin. She was also fiercely loyal, something I knew Edwin valued highly.

I thanked Aaliyah and sat back and enjoyed the soft sofa in the reception area for a few more minutes while I reflected over the last few months. Though a lot of good things had happened, I couldn't help remembering some of the feelings I'd had the first time I'd waited in this same room to share my business plan and dream with Edwin. I wondered why I had put it off for so long. It was interesting how one phone call and a single hour can change your life forever. The phone beeped and Aaliyah smiled and said, "Christian, you can head back. They're ready for you now."

Edwin greeted me with a handshake and a smile. He offered me a seat. Captain James grinned sheepishly and nodded. Edwin said, "I have reviewed all the decisions you've made regarding the crew. I am most impressed, I must say."

I felt a sense of calm and said, "I have been blessed to have you and Captain James help me work through this gauntlet of a task and I want to express my eternal gratitude for your help and the blessings and wisdom each of you have imparted so generously."

"Do you consider Captain James a mentor?" Edwin asked.

"I do," I said.

"The captain feels the same way about you," Edwin said. He looked me in the eyes and continued, "Christian, throughout my life, some of the greatest pain and challenges brought forth the greatest strength and wisdom…if we're open to it. We have another invaluable asset for you. Captain James and I have taken the liberty of asking Michelle, our Human Resources officer to meet with each of your chosen crew members, their families, and next of kin. Captain James and Dwight met with all the crew members after they met with Michelle. Each indicated that it had been a compassionate and positive experience. With that, I believed Michelle would be the right person to keep watch over and act as the liaison between the families, crew members, and the company."

"That's wonderful," I said.

"Christian, I looked over Michelle's credentials," Edwin continued. "She is overqualified for the Human Resource position with her background in human leadership. I recommend you put her on your corporate board as soon as possible. She will be an asset in a multitude of ways. I also think she will bring a unique strength and insight to your board. I feel she has many gifts. Human leadership is only one of them."

"Edwin," I said, "I have given this some thought and would like to add her to the Advisory Board with you and Clayton."

"An excellent decision," Edwin replied. "It makes perfect sense with her responsibilities."

"Christian," Edwin said, "I have been greatly blessed. You are just getting into some of the best chapters of your life. As I look back forty plus years on the wealth I have acquired, I realize that I have been very blessed in a multitude of ways. I see this for you. I cannot buy time nor can I stop it."

He took a breath and continued, "Michelle and Dwight have assigned staff members to each family and have made sure all contracts and HR benefit documents have been approved and that they meet all the compliance guidelines leaving no one behind. So thanks to Michelle, Captain James, and Dwight, you are ready to set sail. Isn't that right, Captain?"

"Yes," said the captain. "You know what Edwin just said about time being a very valuable commodity? Well, he's negotiated a bonus for the retrofitting company. All of the ship's retrofitting and updating including all that we requested will be completed by week's end. This weekend we will do a couple of dry and wet test runs." Captain James then said that if everything checked out safely and successfully, the ship would undergo a final inspection. Once completed, we would receive the appropriate licenses, permits, and certificates that allow our ship to leave the harbor and head into the vast open seas."

There was total silence in the room. The realization of what had just been said shook my very soul. I was overcome with emotion. My dream was unfolding right before my eyes. With unbridled excitement, I looked at Edwin and Captain James. My heart filled with gratitude and I uttered an emotional, "Thank you."

Edwin could see right through me and replied, "Godspeed, Christian. You and Captain James have become *mishpacha* to me."

Edwin said, "Early in my professional career, I believed long hours were the key to success and now that I have a few years on me, I know there are times when long hours may be necessary. One of my mentors had a saying that long hours did not impress him but results did. He knew the true value of time as he had lost a leg to cancer and was still fighting when I worked with him. We have seen the results of years of experience and wisdom. Well done, Captain James and Christian." Edwin continued, "An individual without James's experience could have cost this expedition many more dollars and months with their ship choice. Captain James was an inspired find. Well done, Christian."

I smiled, as did Captain James.

"Now that we have all the final contracts, invoices, licenses, and permit fees," Edwin continued, "my attorney will be in touch with you to honor the deal as discussed." Edwin, then put out his hand to both Captain James and myself.

"Oh, one more thing," Edwin said. "I wanted to discuss gifts with you. There are many more than the twelve I shared with you. Although those twelve have brought me success, there were other influences from which I gained great strength, but the basics always kept my foundation strong and solid. There are other influences that show up from time to time; if they do not integrate into the good gifts, shun them quickly. These are takers of success." Edwin shook his head, as if clearing his thoughts. "Enough of that—let's talk business. Your ship is insured and so are you and the crew; but, there is always risk. Over the last few months we have used real life experience and wisdom to minimize some of the risks, but surrounding yourself with individuals possessing these real-world experiences, gifts, and specialized skill sets will help immensely. I believe you will have success. To what degree, I do not know, because there are many different variations of success. Looking back, I could never imagine not trying, or never taking the chance. Yes, I have drunk from the cup of success, and you will too. Christian, how has this taste of success been so far?"

"I feel a deep inner calling from the seas," I said.

"That is good," Edwin replied. "Christian," he said, smiling.

"This will be another chapter in your life's mission. When you lay a solid foundation for success, you are already in action. Enjoy the motion. You will see that you have progressed greatly." With that, Edwin stood and said, "I will be out of the country for the next week, but you will be too busy to notice. The next time we meet will be on the ship!"

"We would like to christen the ship before shoving off," Captain James said. "And we would like you to do the honor."

Edwin smiled, "I would consider it an honor as well." With that, Edwin gave me a hug and asked if he could do anything else.

"Yes," I said. "I received a call from Linda and the former company merger has turned into a full-blown buyout. Linda would like to increase her initial investment and would like to discuss this as soon as possible. She said I made a wise choice by following my heart. She also said that many of the people and positions were eliminated so they could bring in some of their existing staff from other branches."

Edwin smiled, "I love it when opportunity knocks," he said. "Christian, you have invested the time to build a strong company and corporate team and they are well qualified to handle the transaction. If the terms of the deal are structured correctly, I believe you could have a win-win situation. Timing is everything."

"Yes," I agreed.

"I don't see a problem," Edwin said. "Many times when an individual sets out to change their life, they have to burn a bridge, although I do not advocate for this. I realize in the real world, you either cut bait or go hungry. You know, sink or swim. Christian, I have learned over the years that consulting with a deity has played a major role in the decisions I have made and although I have had my share of disappointments and setbacks in this life, I realize that when I listen to that still, small voice, I am led and given strength to get through those times and further blessed in all things. I know change is hard and most of us have trouble with this from time to time. However, change is a constant in each of our lives. And you've consulted with a higher power through meditation and prayer and this has opened many doors for you. You were able to take a higher road and are fortunate to be able to see some of the possible dividends. Our perspectives and what we build our personal foundation upon will help or hinder the changes we must go through in this journey called life."

Edwin paused for a mysterious moment, looked at me, and said, "Christian, the ship has not even left the harbor and you are seeing abundance flow to you. Had you not followed your heart and calling, not to mention engaging in what you are passionate about, you would have ended up like so many others. Well, I would say this confirms another gift I believe we should all seek; the gift of forever learning. It's been said, Christian, 'let them that would move the world first move themselves.' You ought to try to find a balance somewhere in between. Be forever learning and doing as long as you can. Find the things you love and do those things. Yes, I realize we will all have seasons where this doesn't seem possible. This is where faith becomes the teacher and the great and noble ones will help carry and strengthen you. Yes, Christian, I have a strong belief in them.

"Christian, now that the former president of the company wants to become a financial angel and not a sponsor, I would advise you that in the future a hybrid transaction using debt and equity and possibly some sponsorship might be to your advantage. After all, any time you can reduce your debt, you strengthen your financial positions. Make sure you have the ability to take in other angel investors should you choose. We can discuss this further when I return. You have all that you need at this time as your reserve fund will be even stronger with the increase from Linda."

"Edwin," I said, "I will let Linda know that since she was one of our first sponsors, we are open to her offer of the angel investment capital under a hybrid convertible transaction, which would secure her investment and allow for both a debt and equity position so she could benefit from the interest earned as well as participate in the upside if we are successful. And, we will fully disclose that this is a non-exclusive agreement."

"Once you have made the first discovery and if you are as successful as I believe you will be," Edwin said, "you may not need any additional financial support. However, in minimizing the risk for future ships and expeditions, you may want to do an offering and syndicate the voyage so you can reduce the out of pocket capital and still accomplish what you set out to do. It has always amazed me how much money sits on the sidelines until one has proven themselves. I have continued to cultivate and strengthen my network of individuals. Some were mentors and others helped me launch my business. I was able to help them with their life's work. Christian, when the time comes – and I have a feeling it will soon – lift as many people as you can. It will not always be financial; many times it will not. Be forever lifting just as those who helped and mentored me. You must remember that money is merely a tool, not a requirement to help others rise."

Edwin replied, "I look forward to seeing both of you at the christening and launch in Corpus Christi. Christian," he added, "as you have been learning, faith without works is dead. Action, on the other hand, combined with consistent belief and faith, built on a firm foundation and principles will move you ever closer to your dreams."

I expressed my thanks to Edwin and we exchanged another hug. I shook hands with Captain James and told him I would see him soon. As I walked down the hall and out the door, I felt as I always did after one of our visits. I felt that I had been given more than I had asked for; the sign of a great mentor and teacher.

I had been basking in the moments of each day and trying not to take anything for granted. Being able to embark on a path that I had dreamed of from such a young age filled my soul with love and gratitude.

Speaking of love, as soon as I opened the door to my house, I was knocked to the floor by the force of Sadie's love as she greeted me in her trademark enthusiastic way. I gained my composure and said her three favorite words, "Let's play ball."

She leapt up and grabbed her ball.

I awoke the next morning to a call from Clayton. His voice was full of excitement and vigor. "Christian," he said, "I have made all my travel arrangements with the team and the crew for the launch."

I was ecstatic. "This is more than I ever dreamed of," I said.

"The honor is all mine," he said.

With great humility, I thanked him and let him know how much I was looking forward to seeing him and the rest of my shipmates soon.

I spent the remainder of the time before the launch in final preparation mode. I was trying to balance time with friends and family, while also taking care of the final items on the Gantt chart and task list. Before I knew it, Sadie and I were on our way to catch our red eye flight.

I loaded up Sadie and my luggage and headed to the airport. I calculated that we should make it to our destination in about seven hours. Both Sadie and I settled into a deep, peaceful sleep. It seemed like we'd been dozing for only a few minutes when the flight attendant tapped me on the shoulder to let me know that we were beginning our descent. I was both well rested and excited. In less than an hour, I would meet the team and shipmates and prepare to depart.

I reached down and gave Sadie a good scratch behind the ears. She looked up at me as the plane came in for a landing. I took a moment to look out the window at the bright, sunny day.

Soon, we had our luggage and were on our way to meet the crew. As we approached our destination, I realized I was living a waking dream. I could see the port and the ship rising before us. The car began to slow and I saw Captain James and Clayton along with a few other shipmates. We pulled up next to the dock and Sadie bounded out of the car. I grabbed our luggage and headed towards the waiting ship, ecstatic about what lay ahead for us.

A voyage of many miles begins with one.

12. FINDETH

"WELCOME ABOARD, CHRISTIAN!"

"It's a blessing to be here with you and the crew, Captain James," I said.

"I feel the same way, Christian. We have each been blessed with the gift of a new day and the choice to chart our course in this voyage we call life," said Captain James.

We had gathered in Galveston, Texas at the Port of Galveston for our launch. From there, we would sail into the Gulf of Mexico then into the Caribbean Sea, east of Guatemala and Honduras, then to the west of the Cayman Islands. This was the best location for us to go in search of the proposed Olmec trade routes as mapped and logged by members of Clayton's previous expeditions; these logs, maps, and charts were incredibly detailed. That expedition had also logged and charted two phantom islands; one volcanic in nature and the other lush with dense, tropical vegetation. There were many possible species we might encounter including pit vipers, which are incredibly venomous. We might also find boas, geckos, lizards, turtles, or possibly hundreds of known and unknown species and treacherous terrain.

Faith, hope, and the love of history and the seas had brought each crewmember, the captain, and myself to this place. We found ourselves on a beautiful day filled with salt air and warm sun. We were bathed in nature's beauty.

The Olmecs were the earliest known major civilization in Mesoamerica, dating from as early as 1500 BCE and lasting until 400 BCE. It's believed that they were the first Mesoamerican civilization. The Olmec heartland is in the Gulf lowlands where it expanded after early development in Soconousco Veracruz. The Olmecs were early artisans, collectors, entrepreneurs, builders, and tradespeople known for their talent with basalt, clay, jade, and gold, as well as magnetite and obsidian; leaving a path of historical trade routes and precious art, and a trademark of Olmec colossal heads sculpted from basalt boulders. The civilization had their roots in early farming and would later share their food, water technologies, and sophisticated water routes. The Olmecs are often credited with many first writings, epigraphy, popcorn, and polished mirrors of ilmenite and magnetite. They were diligent traders, moving many of their arts, crops, and collectables by land and sea through merchant trade routes. Some of their treasures were lost at sea while others are believed to be buried on the islands. These treasures are what we were seeking. The more I thought about the Olmec civilization and what we might find, the more excited I became.

Edwin would arrive shortly. All of us felt we had done the best we could to keep our business confidential by heeding the words, "loose lips have sunk many business ships." A driver pulled a nice conservative vehicle into the spot reserved for guests. Edwin had arrived. He smiled as he got out of the car. "Hey, what's the holdup?" he asked as he lit up with a smile.

We went through the ceremonial cutting of the ribbon and breaking of the christening bottle on the hull of the ship to enthusiastic applause. Edwin had a few bites from some of the hors d'oeuvres that had been laid out. Then he said, "I know it's business but take the time to enjoy the journey for there is wisdom in this. You will be all right. Remember who is with you and those who have gone before you. I believe those who have sailed the seas will look after you."

As I was looking out over the ship into the blue and green coastal waves, I felt a hand on my shoulder. I turned and saw a smiling Simon. "The captain would like us all to come below deck for a few minutes," he said. I nodded and followed him; Edwin was close behind.

Over the past month, I'd spent some time getting to know the various members of the crew. They were, to a person, talented, dedicated, and gifted in all the ways Edwin and I had discussed. I was excited to be able to work with them on what could be a momentous journey. I followed the crew member down to the crew mess and found myself standing next to Dr. Bowcutt, the expedition's chief scientist.

Dr. Bowcutt was born into humble beginnings in a small farming community. He loved the outdoors, fishing, his family, and helping others. He'd received his doctorate in his mid-twenties and had continued to excel and mentor others. If he had a weakness, it was his deep and abiding love for baseball and the Angels, currently his favorite team, but above all, he loved a great baseball game. He was a true pioneer and a team asset and he gave credit to his family and deity. He had said several times during the interview process, "We're all here to make a difference." We were lucky to have him aboard.

When the rest of the crew had assembled below deck, Captain James stood before us. He said he had a tradition of offering a captain's blessing and prayer over the ship and crew before every voyage. Captain James indicated that if anyone was uncomfortable and would like not to participate, they were free to leave, but not one crew member left. Everyone was moved by the sincerity of the prayer.

Captain James turned to look Edwin in the eyes. "We will christen the ship, *Levi*," he said, "after your son." Edwin smiled and I saw tears come to his eyes.

Captain James continued, "For those of you who do not know, the name, 'Levi' means 'to bring together.'" Edwin blinked to clear the tears from his eyes. I could see why Captain James had been his captain of choice. Captain James genuinely cared about the success of the crew, ship, and voyage. In everything he said, he never spoke of himself.

"It's time," Edwin said, taking a deep breath to steady himself. "Christian, continue to invest in your crew as each of them has a vast array of priceless experience and knowledge." The expedition had been granted privileged vessel rights due to the historic nature of the voyage. The captain and I walked onto the deck with Edwin, exchanged hugs and handshakes, and watched as Edwin walked down the gangplank, stopped next to his vehicle and in a surreal moment, nodded and waved goodbye.

Then, Captain James' voice echoed across the ship, "All hands to stations!" The engines warmed up, and as if in slow motion, you could see the incredible wake as the ship began to move. As the *Levi* began to glide out of the harbor, I was overcome with emotion. All hands cheered. In a few days, we would arrive at our destination and begin our exploration.

We spent our time on board the ship becoming better acquainted with each other and once again reviewing the current and previous expeditions and historical documents we had compiled. Dr. Bowcutt was working in harmony with Clayton to determine possible sites where we might find artifacts and treasure. Along with the new technology we had available, this would hopefully allow us to become successful in our search. It was reassuring to see the unity between not only Dr. Bowcutt and Clayton, but the entire crew as we progressed on our journey.

In the first week, we had beautiful weather and I could not stop thinking about what might lay before us; I could feel the excitement everywhere I turned. The crew had a robust enthusiasm that everyone could feel. Some of the crew members even thanked me personally for the opportunity, while others kept to themselves; there were a few who made me laugh with their unbridled enthusiasm. Though everyone was professional, some of them had a difficult time keeping the childlike smiles off their faces. We had encountered a few good-sized waves and a few moderate storms but all in all, we were doing well and everyone was in good spirits.

Occasionally I would see Captain James making the rounds with Andrew and Peter. I felt that he was mentoring them on different levels. We had the opportunity to wait out a storm, and the crew put the time to good use. There was some fishing, exercise, and traditional games along with other inspirational activities in our down time. The crew would often play cards or board games or simply sit and talk to each other and get to know one another better.

Time passed quickly and soon we had reached the end of our second week. The vibrant colors of the sunrises and sunsets I saw nearly every day will forever be ingrained in my mind. In my other profession, there were days that I did not want to get out of bed because I was so unenthusiastic about the busy work that faced me at the office, whereas on the ship, I awoke at the same time the sun rose without the aid of an alarm. This might have been a sign that I had found my life's passion and purpose; whatever the reason, the energy and spirit were with me. I only hoped that in some small way, I was sharing that energy and purpose with everyone on the ship.

The next few days were filled with anticipation. The colors of the water changed from dark blues to vibrant teals and white foam, then to light green. Three days before we were scheduled to arrive at our destination, we received news that one of the crew's families had been approached by news media, but had only disclosed that the crew member was at sea. I was thankful for the time being that the time to publicize our voyage had not yet come. We had also received news of a loss; the grandparent of a crew member had died; but in sadness, there was also joy. A baby girl named Gabriella, had been born to the wife of a crew member. I reflected on how interesting it is how we come and go. I thought about the many discussions I'd had with Edwin about the value of time.

The day of our arrival dawned auspiciously. It was a very crisp, beautiful morning; a golden sun crested above the waves on the horizon. There was moisture in the air. After the plan for the day had been established and everyone had been briefed on the day's duties, the exploration began. Between the sonar images, satellite feedback, and the deep-water remote camera, we began to scour the ocean floor for artifacts and treasure. As the first week ended, unfortunately, we had very little to show for our efforts.

At the end of the first week, the Captain asked if we might confer for a few minutes. First mate Andrew took over the ship's bridge so we could regroup. After Captain James listened to my thoughts, he said calmly, "Wealth takes time." He smiled. "We have only been in deep exploration for six days since arriving at the site. I suggest a day of rest," he said. "The anchors have been set, and the weather reports and current conditions suggest very calm and peaceful water and weather. If our infinite and noble creator had a day of rest, I think it's a good idea for all of us!"

"I agree," I said. "It will give us a chance to regroup."

"Over the years and upon different ships and waters," the Captain said, "sometimes we made this a tradition, and those crews who did this far outperformed those that did not."

"That's settled then," I said, and shook Captain James' hand.

I found that the crew members had different ways of spending downtime; however, a lot of them had very similar beliefs and traditions. I understood the wisdom of what Captain James had suggested; it felt right. He said that for essential positions, he would rotate crew members, but all crew would have an opportunity to rest and the chance to renew his or her spirit. I felt immediate peace. Captain James was very wise.

The crew appreciated the downtime. Some members slept, others read, and still others spent the time meditating, but the spirit of peace was with us all. The captain read from a good book and meditated. He told me that he was grateful, but I also noticed that he was the first one back at the helm. I awoke to hear him saying, "Prosperity is found through the inner voice of peace." The modest warmth of the glowing sun permeated each of our beings.

Although the next day we did not bring up any artifacts or worldly treasure, the experience, knowledge, and wisdom I gained were far greater than I could have expected. I felt like a student with some of the best instructors one could ever ask for; a true blessing to be upon the open seas with well-seasoned mentors and shipmates.

It was hard for me to believe that with the most up-to-date equipment and a crew with such specialized knowledge, we were coming up emptyhanded.

Dr. Bowcutt and Clayton recommended we expand our exploration area. Captain James looked up and smiled at them. Andrew said calmly, "Mates, it is time to widen our nets."

The crew seemed to feel sure that if we expanded our search, we would find some indication of success; something to encourage us to continue. The next morning, that is exactly what happened. It's easy to become so focused on the task at hand that you forget to expand your horizons. So it was to be, at the end of our second week of intense exploration, the scanning images indicated there could possibly be artifacts, ship debris, or treasures in the section of exploration depths we were now at. We could feel the excitement, though we only had the pictures. Saturday was to be our first retrieval. We worked through the night and into the next morning. We brought to the surface a few ancient pieces of gold and silver ingots, a few rings, and plates with primitive languages on them; there were pieces of pure gold links that looked as if they were part of larger ones, and other silver relics. The plate material would be determined at a later date. We were in total awe as the team brought up three sealed jars of what appeared to be some kind of kilned pottery.

As Philip cataloged our find, the excitement intensified to the point where everyone was struck silent. We could feel the spirit.

Then, three of the most beautiful coins I'd ever seen were positioned directly in the lens of our deepest camera. It would take an hour or two to bring them in, but the only noise we could hear were the waves breaking against the ship. The anticipation and excitement only continued to percolate with each new find. Captain James and the rest of the crew let out a shout that I swear could be heard halfway around the earth; I am sure even heaven was moved. Over the next few hours, we could feel the spirit of success and history. Shortly, all of our lives would be changed forever.

After the coins were brought on board, Captain James and Dr. Bowcutt said it was time to catalog everything we'd collected and then rest. It had been an exciting day of honest work and the air was cool; night was upon us. The aroma of the warm mess hall meal was carried on the ocean breeze. A small celebration with the crew made for a nice night. Though the excitement was still high, we had been upon the seas for several weeks, and the unity and bonding among the crew was apparent. I could not help thinking about how our lives were changing. We all needed sleep. I headed to my cabin and reflected upon the artifacts and treasure that had been found and the wisdom that those around me had imparted. I took a few moments to meditate and offer a prayer of gratitude. A day of renewal and rest was upon us.

I heard the crew sing a few classics as well as some other inspirational songs. It made for a great close to the evening. We were all exhausted, but the energy and spirit were with us all. As I retired to my quarters, the excitement of the next day was already foremost in my mind. Had I not been so tired, it would have kept me up. But thanks to Captain James, I was learning that some of the greatest strength came through exercise, meditation, prayer, and true rest; the keys to survival and success.

I was the second person awake the next morning. The Captain was always at the stern; I knew that he was rested; he seemed nearly immortal. His drive and passion filled his heart and were evident in everything he did. It's obvious when someone has found their true life's work.

As we reviewed the treasures we'd been fortunate to find the previous day, the sun crested into the navigation room where we stood. Wearing gloves, I picked up each coin carefully and held it in the bright amber rays of the early morning sunshine. The first coin was tarnished; we could see how the elements had acted upon it. The second coin had a little tarnish, but the coloring enhanced its beauty. Unlike the first coin, the second had very little wear. The surface of the coin reflected a bright shine with good historic markings. This coin held a place in history. The third coin, however, took our breath away as the radiant sun gave it a celestial gleam. It shined brilliantly; it was nearly perfect.

The ship had become a vessel of learning; the ocean, a campus; and the crew, an elite group of mentors, professors, and instructors. Abundance, prosperity, and wealth were now upon us. I could not help looking again at that third coin. It felt as if I were looking into something that was of infinite value. Why had it touched my soul so deeply? Only the future would tell.

Expanding our horizons had paid off; we decided to reevaluate and expand the sections of exploration. After we had set our goals, we made moderate adjustments in our exploration. We had success finding artifacts and some ancient treasures. However, just as markets fluctuate, we spent the next week searching but found no additional artifacts or treasure, despite our renewed zeal from the first find.

Although the week went on without finding any additional oceanic artifacts or treasure, the wellspring of the fish and the crew's spirit was amazing. Could we have found all that was to be found? We were in constant contact with Clayton and he encouraged us to stay the course. We had covered all the quadrants of the original search from forty years ago, plus double that. We had passed the halfway mark of our voyage. Time was moving too quickly. That night, I woke remembering the first meeting I'd had with Clayton and the dream he told me about. He'd said that the balance of the treasure was on land; in his dream he had seen artifacts and treasure upon land. I was determined to seek out the closest islands and consult with Dr. Bowcutt. Before I had the chance, I was awakened by a knock on my door. To my surprise, it was Bowcutt himself.

"I have been in contact with Clayton," he said, "and we agree that there is a high probability that additional treasure may be on a neighboring island. We have reviewed what data is available on the two nearby islands. One is mostly volcanic in nature, so it would be almost impossible to excavate. The other is covered with lush vegetation, and the soil conditions could provide an excellent hiding place," he said.

I nodded, thinking that a greater force was at work here.

Since we were not equipped for lava, we chose the second island. We charted the course. It was an estimated seventy nautical miles. The mapping documents that Clayton and his crew had so diligently preserved would now allow the *Levi* and exploration crew to have a pleasant voyage to this once phantom island.

Belief, faith, and persistence bring the harvest of treasures and newfound wealth.

13. AND TO THEM

WE SECURED THE SHIP AND TURNED THE *LEVI* TO CRUISE WITH THE current instead of against it. The course was set, and as long as the water remained smooth, it would only take a few hours to reach our destination. This would be a few memorable nautical miles. I could feel the crew's excitement, and after a few weeks at sea, I welcomed the thought of land.

Captain James moved the ship smoothly across the deep blue and green water. The brisk, salty breeze was refreshing and we were excited about what we might find. Previous finds had only increased our enthusiasm for what might come. If anything, we were increasingly excited. I had heard many times that one should enjoy the journey on the way to success and recommit to be forever learning in order to fully progress. The sound of the breaking waves, the mist of the ocean, and the warmth of the sun was breathtaking. My heart was focused on the mission and the crew and I learned to find joy in the present moment.

I rarely saw Captain James far from the bridge, and when I did, he was walking with Andrew or Peter. He always had a slight grin on his face. I never saw him sluggish or sad, and the limp from the cancer seemed to fit his character; he looked as dapper and seasoned as a leader could be.

I spoke with Captain James and Dr. Bowcutt, and together we estimated that we would drop anchor about a nautical mile from shore. This was the best and likely most successful way to get the crew to shore using a few of our hovercrafts as there were no ports on the island and it was uninhabited.

We were about an hour away when we began to get a glimpse of what was to come. It was a picture-perfect setting, usually re-served for dreams. Everyone was watching our approach closely. The Captain reduced speed, and the ship was breaking the waves. The only noise was the vibration of the ship, but it was music to our ears. We glided across the blue-green water as if we were on glass. The waves were so transparent, we could see the ocean floor.

We were minutes away, and the ship slowed. Across the deck, we heard the shout, "Drop anchor!" There was a loud cranking noise, then a giant splash on both sides of the ship as the anchors were dropped. The ship was ready for the crew to cast off, and the Captain's voice shared the long-awaited message: "All land lovers and all hands report to the deck!" A few of the crew members lowered the hovercrafts that would take us to shore. One of the hovercrafts would be instrumental in carrying all the necessary camp and exploration equipment to the island. The other would serve as the go-between for the crew members and additional necessary tools. All of us would set foot on dry land tonight, and we agreed that we would build a fire and have dinner on the island, as long as it was deemed safe. A few of the crew knelt on the ground when the hovercraft brought them safely to land; kissing the ground was a longtime tradition. By the time dusk arrived, we had identified and mapped several sections for the next few weeks of exploration. We also identified some of the vegetation and we were visited by some very aggressive, colorful, and curious reptiles, a few known skinks, and some species known only to the island. We took a few pictures and noted them for later observations and study. The crew dug a fire pit on the beach, and other crew members set up a temporary shelter for equipment that would be unloaded early the next day. It was time for a fire and dinner.

The fire began with a small spark, then a few minutes later, the flames grew. The warmth spread, and then a wonderful, brilliant light filled the area—our home away from home. The smoke seemed to speak a language of its own. Golden embers floated out to sea, and childhood memories of campfires came to mind. After dinner, the crew gathered around the fire to go over the plans for the next few days. I was intrigued by each of their contributions and gifts. I was fortunate to be able to feel their strength. I was also enthralled by the unity, leadership gifts, and traits they each shared and utilized as an elite crew and team. In the cool island air, we found warmth, not just by fire, but the spirit of the conversations and stories we told warmed our souls. As the smell of burning wood permeated our senses and the golden yellow, orange, and red embers provided radiant heat and light, we were each edified in our own special way.

Going into the night, the crews' conversations turned to bucket list items as well as individual and collective goals, missions, and targets. It was the gift of timing; being in the right place at the right time, I was being fed in a way that my intellect and spirit would take with me through eternity. As the night was winding down, Captain James shared a personal story of how it was his belief that in great times and in times of trial, he had learned those that had gone before us either on land or sea looked out for us as we continued to move our life's work and purpose forward. He then added, "In order to know this, you will all have to experience it and I know each of you will."

With that, John added a few more pieces of wood to the fire as if to say that we should remember this evening. We all had a great purpose and would be helped beyond ourselves to accomplish what we believed in.

Andrew and John both expressed gratitude to Captain James for his inspiring words. The sounds of the ocean and the smell of both the smoke from the fire and the salty air created an ambiance of excitement on a level I had never experienced. It was as though everyone felt that all things were possible. Everyone was focused on the most positive things; some of a spiritual nature.

Even though it would be our first night sleeping on the island and all of the crew were extremely tired, we could feel a special island spirit. None of us wanted the night to end, but knowing how much work was ahead of us the next day, we found our place of solitude and rest.

The next morning came quickly, but everyone felt rested and ready. The Captain, true to form, was at the bridge reporting in and filing future plans for the navigation home. I could never outpace him; it was obvious that he loved what he did and the crew knew it.

It was apparent that Captain James was living his best life and it showed in each of us. He was a leader, mentor, and teacher. He felt his life and those around him were all integrated into his journey; he'd had failures and was able to learn and grow from them but they were only part of who he had become. His commitment and passion to his life's work allowed him to inspire and lift others which I know was further strengthened by his honesty and integrity. He walked in the path of accountability of himself as well as those around him. He constantly allowed others to learn and grow and he helped them rise seeing sometimes what others had not seen in themselves. I believe that his life was built upon solid principles and values as his confidence was strong, not just in himself, but in those whom he walked and worked with. I believe that to all whom he loved, he was a true leader and mentor. I was learning from him that meekness should never be mistaken as weakness. I am sure if needed, James could call down the thunder. He was full of passion and life and possessed true greatness.

As the work began, Dr. Bowcutt, a few crew members, and myself brought out and strategically positioned the detectors, other equipment, and sensors. We were able to scan and image the subsurface with a fair amount of success to a depth of about eight feet and up to twelve feet in some areas, or, as the captain would say, two fathoms. With imaging data of this section, it was decided by Dr. Bowcutt and Clayton that this would be a low depth excavation limited to a few specific areas. Working with such highly gifted and skilled individuals was proving invaluable. Their educations and experiences had already proved key to the expedition's success and with great anticipation, and a deep feeling of elation, the next chapter of treasure seeking and exploration was well underway.

I could see belief and hope even in Thomas's face. Philip was ready to open and catalog any new and ancient archeological discovery or find. But after the first few hours, we had a discovery; another artifact which appeared to be a carving of an intense dark green imperial jade eagle.

The day seemed to go by quickly. I was convinced that when you do what you love, that is how it sometimes goes. As the day pressed on we unearthed a figurine-like sculpture in jade. Upon closer examination, this rare emerald green piece of jade would be of the highest points in the artifact grading world; a true treasure. It may have been sculpted after a person of dignity or royal status, as a princess or queen. Myself and the other crew members felt it was close to the same era as our ocean floor discoveries.

After the find, we realized that there was a reason that Clayton had the dreams he'd had. His work was not complete and although Clayton was not on the island with us, he was here in guidance, intellect, and spirit. His crew's work laid a solid foundation for the future and we were part of that future. I was beginning to really see that when you put a dream into action and make every effort with consistent progress and planning, it begins to come to pass. Yes, we were on the verge of greatness and had opened the door to prosperity and wealth. Something inside me said, "This is only some of what I have in store for each of you."

We had only covered a small portion of the island when, almost one hundred paces from the last find, we discovered another. Soon, we unearthed a thick gold ingot, and then we discovered a goblet that appeared to be made of pure silver.

There were about three hours of daylight left. The beauty that surrounded us was surreal; there were lush tropical vines and trees in many shades of green. It was truly a mecca of paradise. Suddenly, a loud yell burst from a member of the crew; another beautiful piece had been found! This one was a gem of the purest cut; a ruby surrounded by an array of smaller stones. It was a magnificent piece; it was very rare for the Olmec era and had possibly been crafted for nobility.

We had a visit from a few pythons which was a little nerve-racking, but what would a day be without a little danger? I thought of the Captain's prayer; knowing that we were being looked after in many ways. I heard Clayton's words: "The treasure you seek will probably be found on the island." The day was nearly over and we'd found extremely valuable artifacts and treasure, both from a historical and monetary perspective.

We arrived at base camp, where a report of our findings and a quick cataloging and debriefing took place. An aroma of evening island grilling drifted through the air. It was time for the crew and I – and Sadie – to make the most of the evening. Sadie had not only been a great shipmate, but she had formed a bond with the crew and had been enjoying her time with Captain James, as well as exploring the island. Sadie and the crew and I were all hungry in a multitude of ways. Foods for the body, mind, and spirit were only a few steps away.

After dinner, I received a message from Edwin: "I hope that all is well and I appreciate the update. After speaking with Clayton, he advised us to look in areas that, if you were under attack, you would go for protection and shelter and where you would bury the treasure. I think the Olmec's tradesmen or pirates may have been attacked on the island and hidden their treasure. Godspeed, my friends, captain, and crew."

Once again, the crew and fire fueled one another; however, on this night they discussed their goals and dreams, as if the ultimate treasure had already been unearthed. They were already visualizing their individual success, and for the first time, this sent chills down my spine. I had heard many times that if you help enough people get what they want, you will end up with what you desire as well. What a true gift it is to be surrounded by greatness.

The sun seemed to rise even more quickly the next morning.

Captain James had his crew members up before dawn. The smell of a campfire cooking breakfast permeated through the air. Heeding the words of the message I'd received from Edwin the previous night, we decided that the new quadrant of exploration would involve lush areas of deep cover as well as trees and wooded areas. There was one particular area where the trees were much older than the treasure we sought. As I looked at these beautiful and magnificent creations, the size of their roots, and the ways they intertwined with one another, I remembered one of the moments I'd had with Captain James when he'd told me, "You will need deep roots to weather the storms of life."

We noticed that in this part of the island, the ground cover was softer than in other areas. Patches of sunlight shone through the canopy of leaves. After a day of work, we called it quits. The crew took care of dinner as well as some entertainment. With Sadie at my side, I settled in and grabbed my guitar to play some of the crew's favorites. James and John began singing and soon others chimed in while others danced. A full moon lit the skies, making the ocean glow brilliantly in her subtle white light. The next day would come quickly.

In the morning, I was awakened by a crew member's voice. I went over to see what was going on, and some of the crew were going over the imagery that our equipment had documented. There was an area with a glowing image over it about eight feet below the surface. When I refocused the screen, I found it was from a deep part of the tree grove—either an equipment malfunction or a sign of success. "Let's get things prepared for a test hole," I said. It took about an hour to locate and assemble the test bits and the specialized core drill. The sun was cresting and I helped the cook get breakfast started; soon the smell of fresh island fruit, grilled island fish, and potato pancakes, or latkes, floated through the air. We had outpaced Captain James for the first time on this journey; he smiled and thanked us for breakfast.

"Can you feel it?" he asked.

"What?" I asked him.

"There's something in the air—a feeling," he said. "You can't voyage as many years as I have without having a sense; it's a gift, I guess. I feel it; greatness and success are closer than we know." Captain James paused for a moment before speaking again. His words touched my soul. "Christian, when I was forced to retire early due to the Big C, it was very difficult for me. But I have deep roots in my faith and the great and noble ones, and that gave me the strength to triumph over my affliction. But there is more I feel you need to hear. You gave me the opportunity to share this extraordinary expedition regardless of my age; I am grateful to be here with this amazing crew and you. This gave me a renewed purpose and restored my dignity, not to mention the dream of being on the open seas again. There is untold strength in an achievable and righteous cause or dream and for this I am eternally grateful."

I was so overcome with emotion, all I could do was offer him a hug and let him know that I felt equally blessed and grateful.

"Yes, I feel it too," I said.

"Christian, if your time was shorter than you thought, what would you do? Just stand here or get done what you came here to do?"

"Captain James, you already know the answer. You get it done."

With that, Captain James gave me a genial clap on the shoulder and looked at me with his deep blue, wisdom-filled eyes and said, "I believe you're right, but I sense a little hesitation. Remember, Christian, when we are on the verge of greatness, it's fear that tries to keep us from all that the great and noble ones have in store for us. You have shown faith ever since I met you, but brother, now is the time to forever walk by faith. I made this decision when I was about your age and it has served me well and those I serve well. Go by faith and do what you were meant to do for in this, you will be blessed."

After breakfast, my intuition took hold. I had heard that great athletes used the term "throwing blind," when they developed an inner trust in themselves and their team as well as the inherent belief in what was possible. I needed to let go and see with my spiritual eyes what divinity had planned. This was hard for me, but it was necessary for all of us. After reviewing the results of the current boreholes. I saw we were bringing up a scented wood of some kind. It appeared to be ancient oak, coated in a material that gave off a musty smell; it smelled like success. We had put the framework into place for a deeper excavation of this selected section.

As I looked up, I saw Peter and Thomas; I greeted them both and heard Thomas ask, "Do you really think there is any more treasure to be found on such a remote place on earth?" I paused for a moment and saw Peter put his arm over Thomas' shoulder.

Without hesitation, Peter replied, "Thomas, have we not seen the hand of providence upon each of us on this very expedition? Then why do you doubt?"

Thomas replied, "Peter, yes I have seen the hand of prosperity and providence and know we have already been blessed greatly and I know we are not here out of greed but a true desire to do what we have been called and tasked to do."

With that, Peter turned to me and said, "Christian, I can only tell you that my heart is pounding with anticipation of what may be discovered. If we have already discovered all that there may be on this expedition, each of us has already prospered greatly for making the journey."

I looked at both Peter and Thomas and let them both know that I felt the same way and would be forever grateful for their friendship and constant guidance, help, and knowledge. With Peter, Thomas, and Sadie by my side, we set out to meet up with the crew for a very exhilarating and momentous day.

We should be ever mindful of those who are placed in our lives; we must ensure they truly have our best interests at heart.

14. THAT KNOCKETH

WE TOOK SOME TIME TO ASSESS THE CORE MATERIALS WE HAD brought up. The samples were laid out carefully under a tent near the dig, protected from the bright sun, wind, or rain. The oak-like cores were thoroughly saturated with a substance that smelled strongly of wax. It seemed to have been used as a sealant against the elements. Clayton and Dr. Bowcutt estimated that it would take about eight hours to reach the detected and scanned items below the subsurface soils. We wanted to approach the dig from an archeological standpoint, rather than as a simple extraction of earth and materials. Preserving the find was key. If we destroyed it, not only would it lose its intrinsic value, but we would be destroying history where our hope was to preserve it.

With the exploration well underway, a feeling of excitement rolled over each of us in turn. The crew found a few tools, a sword, and an old knife. Philip was very detailed in the cataloging of all the artifacts and treasures that were being discovered, being sure to keep moving at the careful pace we had set. The crew was elated; I would see a smile from time to time or hear an excited exchange between team members. Captain James reiterated that although anticipation was high, he could feel the spirit of what was at hand. With his words, I felt the utmost respect and reverence descend upon the crew.

The crew made good use of our time; a few hours into the dig, a honey and spicy wax smell began to flow to the surface. This smell only increased our desire to see what could possibly be buried at this excavation site. Sharing time in the trench was necessary so that all could take a break from time to time; each crew member working in unity had the chance to participate as they relieved each other on a rotating schedule. I don't think that any of us expected what was about to be found; a fully intact ancient piece of history. It was a very old, sealed, wooden chest of perfect size and structure. This one appeared to have some type of inscription across the top. We used a light brush to clean the surface, dusting away the final layer of dirt. We took photographs and examined them, determining the best way to go about opening our find. We excavated each side of the chest to give ourselves plenty of room to open the top. We feared the entire chest might disintegrate if we attempted to hoist it all at once; so we proceeded with an abundance of caution.

All the crew members would witness such a phenomenal and historical moment as we each knew that this was only possible due to each member's contributions and the extended hand of providence.

It was time. The rusted old pins were carefully removed from the four corners of the top. Carefully and in unison, we lifted the treasure chest lid. The old, waxy smell was soon overtaken by a spicy honey and vanilla fragrance. What had we found? Peter looked at the inside of the chest lid and said, "This carving looks like a hummingbird. I recognize this wood. I believe it's called sacred oak."

Old material lay on top of the chest; it looked to be pieces of bedding and clothing. One piece at a time was carefully removed. I had the honor of removing the last piece of cloth. There was only silence at what we saw before us. I looked forward to the singing of the tropical island birds and the sightings of the colorful local animals moving about in the island vegetation. As the salty ocean trade winds blew, it caused a spinning of tree leaves and a rushing and whistling noise could be heard throughout the island.

This was a sweet spot in time, as history was being written. I looked over what we had found and at the faces of the crew members. I could see that each had a celebratory demeanor.

John asked what I thought of all that had been found. I was honest and replied that I was overwhelmed. "It's greater than what I had imagined." John just smiled.

Philip then said, "After logging these additional finds, Christian, I feel that much more than priceless treasure have been discovered on this voyage."

I felt a chill, then a tingle of warmth as the island sun caused a peace to flow through me. I believe this was what was known as pure elation.

I could see gratitude in the face of each crew member. I only hoped they could see the same in mine. We had been guided to help Clayton see the balance of his dream become a reality and in return, he had been instrumental in helping us achieve our dreams. We looked into the chest and saw stacks of coins, various colored stones, goblets, chains, and pearls! The hands of providence had graced us.

In the corner of the chest were many gold coins as well as large ingots. There were small nuggets of gold and twelve beautiful vases of an alabaster color. There was also another box that looked to be made of silver, and when I opened it, there were twenty-seven ancient gold and silver coins inside. Another smaller vase of an ivory material contained thirty-nine similar coins. They differed in historical dates but were all very beautiful.

In one corner of the chest was a stack of plates; we counted fifteen in all. There was a material dating from ancient times that was fastened like a handbag; it fit in the palm of my hand. As I loosened the top of the material, I saw the most beautiful sight. Inside were stunning pearls with a blue and silver sheen. I opened the bag and the sunlight shone off the pearls. They varied in size; we counted 138 in all.

A smaller bag of similar cloth was located at the bottom of the original bag, and it, too, contained large pearls of different colors; there were five of these and each was extraordinarily beautiful.

We found another golden box; however, after cleaning it a little, it appeared to be made of brass. I opened it slowly so as not to damage it. The box seemed to be lit from within; several white, clear stones glowed. I took one in my hand, and it looked as if I was holding the sun at noon. We counted and cataloged them as we had done with everything else. There were sixteen of these bright stones.

It was approaching dusk; we had, at best, an hour of light left. Half of the crew had taken what had been found thus far and loaded it onto the ship; the other half remained with me at the dig. The old oak treasure chest was nearly empty. We removed the rest of the material cautiously. There was another alabaster type of container containing fifteen ancient gold coins. Each one was engraved with a different message. There was also a wooden box with a top containing an inscription that would need to be translated. The leather straps holding the top were mostly decayed. As we removed the top slowly, an awe came over the majority of the crew as we gazed upon three possible Olmec vases, each depicting artistic work of people and flowing water. They were absolutely breathtaking. A tube contained a small leather roll that had not been moved by the elements of time or weather. Upon review, it appeared to be a map of where there might be additional artifacts or treasures from the same period.

Crew members worked to transport the finds safely to the ship as others worked to restore the dig site. Dr. Bowcutt suggested we play a game of island baseball in celebration of the gifts of each other and the success of the voyage.

"Count me in," I heard Simon respond. "I'll bring James back to play as well."

Peter and Andrew said they were up for a game and Matthew agreed as well. Before I knew it, we had enough players for a full game.

Once the artifacts and treasures had been secured and cataloged on the ship, it was game time. Dr. Bowcutt had secured a few palm leafs and a few sizable angel oak branches for use as benches. He smiled as he reached into his duffle bags and pulled out a few baseballs,bats and gloves. Then he, Philip, and Thomas set island palm leafs out to mark the bases.

Teams were selected and I heard Peter yell, "Let's play ball!"

We played our best approximation of baseball, laughing, running, catching, and fielding in the island sand. The sun began to set giving way to an absolutely stunning evening. Simon hit a home run in the dying light. Soon after, Captain James found himself at the plate. He fouled off the first pitch, a knot in the tree branch catching the baseball at an odd angle and sending it flying off into the forest. When the next pitch came, I knew before he even hit it; it was a home run. As the Captain made his way slowly around the bases and across home plate, his face radiated pure joy. A fitting way to end the game.

Afterwards, we gathered around the campfire to enjoy the warmth and reminisce. Peter looked over at Captain James and asked, "Captain, would you say life is a lot like baseball?"

Without hesitation, the Captain replied, "Certainly. There will be times in each of our lives where we strike out, other times we get to first or second, and occasionally third. And, sweetest of all, a triumphant home run. I have learned the bases are like milestones in life. And your team, are those who you run and walk the path with; including family, friends, teachers and all those who have mentored you. In baseball, when up to bat, each pitch represents possibility and opportunity. In life, each day can do the same. But, it is up to us to choose how and what we do with that gift. At times each of us may feel like we're stuck waiting in the dugout forever; always in practice or sidelined, but never getting into the game. It is important to remember that these are the times to prepare, to grow and to heal.

"It may take some time, but the most important thing is to focus on being ready for what may come your way. When you're called, you need to be ready. Know your playbook and most importantly, stay in the game. No matter how many times you strike out, you must get back up, get on deck, and keep swinging. Put the ball in play, and then you will find your success."

"I couldn't have said it any better. We appreciate what you have shared with us, Captain."

The remaining crew members loaded up the last few items on the island and headed to the hovercraft so they could return to the ship.

I caught up with Dr. Bowcutt. "You just happened to have baseball equipment with you?" I asked.

He smiled, "The bats and gloves were a gift from a loving grandfather and dear baseball friend; they are rare collectibles," he said. "I take them with me as they have always brought me good luck, good memories, or both." He held a bat and one of the gloves up for me to see—they were amazing.

"What does it say?" I asked, noticing some faint writing on the leather.

"I'll share that at a later time," he replied, "When the time is right." Bowcutt then held the glove so I could take a closer look. "The G. Wassil is a rare glove," he responded. "Only a few Bowcutt Blaster bats are known to exist."

"What incredible gifts," I said.

He nodded in agreement. "You are right, Christian," he replied.

As the hovercraft skimmed across the beautiful ocean, a light salty spray invigorated my senses causing an inspirational stirring of my soul.

As we boarded the ship with the balance of the crew, there was a modest feeling of accomplishment that radiated throughout the ship. A delightful aroma filled the ship. As dinner began, it was a time to give thanks, to reminisce, and to live in the moment. It was serendipitous and we were filled with joy and appreciation for what we had been able to accomplish together. This was to be our last night anchored near the island before we navigated out to sea for the journey home.

After dinner, many of the crew members retired early; it had been a rewarding but exhausting day. I found myself on the bridge with Captain James and expressed my gratitude to him and gratitude from the crew. Each of us wanted him to know that he was appreciated and valued. I told him about the artifacts and treasures we had found and expressed our genuine love for him. His experience and insight had been imperative to our success. "Christian," he said, "I greatly appreciate all that you and the crew have shared with me. We have all been blessed in a multitude of ways." He continued, "Over the years, I have come to know some of mine and that I am only a steward of the use of these gifts for good," he said. "We will pull anchors at sunup!" Captain James smiled, hugged me, and said each individual lives a lifetime not necessarily measured in years. "Christian," he said, "before you retire below, I feel impressed to share with you something I have found to be of great truth and worth to me. In each of our lives, there will come a time that we have to draw on strength beyond what we possess, and the strength of others, for it will be the only way to accomplish what the great and noble ones have in store for you. It is part of a divine plan. Don't ever hesitate when you need this help and strength."

"How will I know?" I asked.

Captain James replied, "Trust these words and you will know."

I retreated to my cabin, contemplating what it would be like when we arrived home. Things had changed and I felt in every way that our lives were going to be different. That night I prayed for everyone and asked that I be given strength and granted the wisdom to handle the changes in my life and allow me to be a wise steward.

I awoke to the anchors being pulled from the seas. The word *purpose* kept coming to mind. I was greeted by the morning sun warming my face. Breakfast had begun. John reviewed all of the return navigation plans. The return travel plans for the *Levi* had been approved and received; we were headed back to the open seas.

The first three days of our return voyage were very calm. The sun was either shining or we had partial clouds and light rain. Upon being updated about our future weather conditions, the captain had asked Peter and Andrew to let the crew know of the storm brewing so everyone would have time to prepare before we were under siege and at the mercy of the weather.

Captain James had been advised to stay the course, as the other possible routes were already too dangerous for safe passage. After consulting with the closest navigation center and Coast Guard, we had no choice but to push forward as there was no chance to turn back. While green and dark grey clouds filled the sky, we had received strong warnings about possible danger to the crew and ship. We were at the mercy of the great and noble ones and the vast, open seas.

For the first time during the voyage, we heard a change in the Captain's voice. The crew was updated. Each of us worked to prepare the ship for the approaching storm. All that could be covered, fastened, and secured safely under storm protocol was underway. We all worked in harmony to implement the safeguards to the best of our ability. Increasingly rough waves pounded the ship on all sides, the *Levi* was on high storm alert by that evening.

Everyone was exhausted, but the thought of returning home motivated the crew to find peace and rest. The night brought a heavy darkness. Along with Captain James, we rotated watch and took care of our assigned stations so that all crew members could get some rest. As dawn approached, we were awakened by heavy rain. It reminded me of a helicopter ride from years past when I'd visited the waterfalls on the island of Kauai. Each crew member was at their respective stations. With the brisk gust of wind, there was a break in the rain and we could feel the sunshine trying to break through the dark cloud cover. I heard the captain say, "We're in the eye of the storm; it's not finished yet." Unfortunately, he was right. A heavy, torrential downpour was soon upon us.

We all heard Captain James' voice: "It will be all right." No sooner had we heard those words than a huge wave crested over the bow.

We were in the fight of our lives and all we could do was hang on and do our part to look out for each other. Just breathing and clearing our eyes took nearly everything we had. As relentless as the storms of life can be, we found ourselves engulfed and partially submerged in another king-sized wave. Our large ship suddenly seemed impossibly small. I prayed from my heart, *God help us all!*

It's interesting how one's perspective of time can be altered so quickly. What felt like an eternity lasted less than a minute. When the wave hit, we felt the vibration throughout the entire ship; the ship groaned in agony. Then, like cresting a hill on a roller-coaster, a capsizing feeling rushed over me as the *Levi* took such an extreme descent. Captain James took the hardest hit. All the ship windows in the bridge were blown out and most of the windows below deck were gone. The *Levi* was taking on an enormous amount of water in its lower decks.

Andrew and I went to the bridge to assist Captain James. As I was taking in the condition of the Captain and the bridge, I heard Simon yelling for Peter, "Take cover and hold on!" When I turned back around, I saw what Captain James and the others were looking at; another wave headed straight for the *Levi*. Captain James would not let Andrew take over. Instead, he put him to work assisting at the bridge. The Captain yelled, "It's a rogue wave! Oh, have mercy on our souls!" Once again, I felt the ship groan in agony.

It felt as if time were standing still and in those moments, my life certainly flashed before my spiritual eyes. I am sure I was not alone in this. I offered a silent prayer for the entire crew and their loved ones and asked God to send His protection and guardian angels. How could such beauty and calmness change so swiftly to deliver a storm that put us in a fight for our temporal lives?

Once the wave had passed and the ship had righted itself, we conducted a head count and crew check. Thomas was missing and a call went out, "Man overboard!"

Then we heard Simon exclaim, "I see him! He's portside!"

In an instant, we saw Matthew and Simon throw him the lifeline flotation devices. Thomas had one behind him and one in front of him. Then he was fully submerged again. The rough water rolled over the top of Thomas and for a moment, he was out of sight. Then, as if divine help had favored him, there he was in the deep ocean with his right hand grasping one of the flotation devices. Simon, Matthew, and Peter began to bring him back shipside. They were able to get Thomas back onto the ship's deck and, as he began to regain his senses, he collapsed briefly.

After a few moments, he regained his composure and began to speak. "I have been part of a miracle today," Thomas explained. "I thought I was surely going to die. I went under several times and all I could think of were the words of Captain James, how each of us will have times where we will need to draw on strength beyond our own. I had faith in his words and now have first-hand experience of the wisdom he has been sharing with us."

Peter replied, "Thomas, there are times in each of our lives where we will need to be rescued. What is important is that we always remember that we were. Then one day, we will be able to pay it forward. I was never the same after almost being engulfed by the sea, but the change that came over me made me who I am today. There is no shame in being saved by grace."

"Yes, Thomas," Simon said. "Captain James has in his own wise way, been imparting invaluable knowledge and some of his experiences in order to prepare and strengthen each of us so that we may do the same for others and be able to bless the lives of others, just as he has done for us." With that, the majority of the crew members began working to remove excess water from the ship.

With all the power out, a darkness had come over the ship. The majority of the emergency equipment onboard was submerged below deck. As the storm began to subside and the skies began to glow, a light transmitted through the antiquated deck prism and provided sufficient light for the diligent crew to see well enough to get the pumps working. We all worked hard to return the water to the sea.

When all but a foot or so of water remained, I was asked to meet with Andrew, John, and Matthew at the ship's helm. Once there, I was also greeted by the ship's doctor, Nathanial, who met me with a distraught expression. Captain James had remained at the helm looking the worse for wear. He had taken a severe beating. Andrew and Matthew had stepped in with Nathanial to relieve the Captain of command. Yet, Captain James had told them he was not finished. A short while and a few nautical miles later, he looked out at the water, a look of eternity filled his deep blue eyes and smiled. "We are in safe water now," he said. He allowed himself to be led to his quarters where he collapsed. Fortunately, Captain James' cabin was one of the dry ones. Nathanial and John would administer to James throughout the night. Sadie refused to leave his side. Captain James would abide in the arms of mercy and grace.

We all felt the sadness of what had happened. We kept ourselves busy by cleaning and repairing what parts of the ship we could. We worked through the night, and about fifteen minutes before sunrise, by unspoken agreement, we gathered in front of the door to Captain James' quarters.

Nathaniel pulled me aside and whispered, "It is only by a miracle that he's still alive." A smile from James took some of the heaviness out of the room, but it was brief.

With tears flowing from his sea-weathered blue eyes, Captain James looked upon each of us with a final look and spoke these words: "I have loved each of you and each of you are destined for greatness. Be believing and fear not. Please give a hug to my wife and daughters when you see them and give each of them my love. Let them know I will be there constantly keeping watch. Now go forward with faith. Until we meet again." With those last words, a beautiful, almost indescribable spirit of peace and love followed by a sense of warmth engulfed each of us then filled his cabin and flowed across the weathered ship.

In that moment, we all knew James had graduated from this mortal life with distinctive high honors and was awaiting his next voyage at heaven's door.

In the face of adversity came forth a divine spirit of courage and strength to carry us forward.

15. IT SHALL BE OPENED

GREATER LOVE HATH NO MAN THAN THIS, THAT A MAN LAY DOWN HIS life for his friends. Yes, Captain James was a dear and true friend and he had insured our well-being and left each of us a divine level of hope that we would be able to complete our journey and return to those who were depending on us. His confidence was infectious perhaps because he did not harp on it; he was simply a leader, you felt as though all things were possible in his presence. When the captain wasn't at the bridge, he was guiding us in some other area of life. He was a true mentor and teacher. Even though our hearts were heavy, we would carry on in the spirit of honor and optimism as a tribute to our friend. We had carried forward with the maintenance and service of the ship; it would require all of us to work in unity, drawing on each other's gifts and strengths. At the same time, we were being sustained and given the fortitude to work through the night to help further prepare the ship for the voyage home.

In the warmth of the rising sun the next morning, we found an increased feeling of hope and a renewal of life and spirit. I could not help thinking that even though Captain James was not physically with us, he had outpaced us yet again by helping bestow such a beautiful sight upon each of the crew.

Radiant orange, gold, and yellow hues of the sun graced the ship with the renewal of another day; a magnificent gift to come out of the darkest of nights and into a blue bright, sun-filled, and peaceful day. It was with open hearts, the crew would prepare for the services of Captain James and to honor his request to be buried at sea.

All hands had prepared for the service. After opening with a prayer, we sang one of James's favorite sea shanties, "'Tis Our Sailing Time." As we reached the fourth verse and sang the words, "When my time is over, Haul away for Heaven, Haul away for Heaven, God be at my side," a feeling of a life well-lived permeated my very soul.

Each crew member shared a thought or memory of the captain. When it was my turn, I shared the story of meeting him on my flight to Colorado. I hadn't known it at the time, of course, but the meeting had been serendipitous and because of it, much of what we had accomplished had been possible. Peter walked to the front and wiped the tears from his eyes. He began to speak.

"Over the years of serving Captain James," he said, "He indicated that possibly one day, one of us would be speaking on behalf of the other. He gave me an envelope and somehow it survived the storm. I have been on the seas many times with Captain James and never have I seen waves of the magnitude we experienced. I open this envelope on behalf of each of you." He paused for a moment, carefully pulling out a single sheet of paper. He read:

"Dear crew,

If you are listening to Peter read these words, then my mission here upon this Earth is complete. I would ask each of you to live your best life each and every day. I am aware that sometimes this is difficult, so please believe there is a lot of good yet to come. Over the years I found that I had many weaknesses but with the correct principles and a solid foundation built on deity and a higher purpose, I was able to turn a lot of those weaknesses into some of my greatest and most rewarding strengths. I have no doubt that each of you have already done this and will continue to do so. There will be times in each of your lives that you may find that the great and noble ones have greater faith in you than you have in yourself. That is when prayer, meditation, and real opportunities for growth will come.

"Much like the waves of the sea, when those times of adversity come and go, be forever learning and forever serving, as I have had the privilege of serving with each of you. You are leaders in your own respective fields. I have personally witnessed this and the many other gifts, skills, and talents you have each been blessed with. For that is one of the many blessings of this mortal journey. We each come with a multitude of gifts, skills, and talents and how we multiply and use them is up to us.

"In my life's journey, I have tried to use them in an honorable way and to make a difference for good. I know each of you will continue to do the same. Surround yourselves with those whom you love and with those who love you as this is one of the most powerful gifts there is. I know this love and it has brought forth the miracles I have seen and been part of. Hope is also very powerful and one of the definitions I have come to understand that hope for me meant helping other people excel. You will see some of the choicest and greatest blessings come to pass in this life and the life to come if you are one who believes. Now, go forward and take care of your vessel and know that God will prevail.

"I leave you now, but only for a season. We will see each other again. Know that I am with you all the way. Make a difference for good with the time you have and take good care of your ship and each other."

It was a surreal moment. All of us were better individuals for having been a part of James' life. We returned him to the sea with honor. We stood silent for a moment followed by a full sound-off; we could hear the shots roll across the seas. Captain James had lived out his dreams, followed his heart and passion, possessed incredible gifts, and used them to profoundly and truly make a difference for good. Even though James' physical presence was at rest, we knew we were not alone in this next chapter of life and each of the crew members had indicated that following the services, they were overcome with emotion. They too, knew they were not alone and it was time to keep moving forward as that is what both their loved ones and

James would want for each of them. Now was the time for the crew to unite and something deep inside let each of us know that James was somehow with each of us. Each of the crew members indicated after the services that they felt they were being looked after in a very peaceful and protective way. It was very surreal. I am sure the captain had a hand in it.

It was a time of great focus and each crew member would reassess the communication equipment, the ship's condition, and fuel and food reserves.

There was a slightly salty, warm breeze. The crew was on deck to meet with Peter, our Captain, and to render the *Levi's* condition. It was determined that all communication equipment had been destroyed by the storm and the majority of cell and satellite antennas and transmitters were also destroyed. The radios were saturated beyond restoration and all the ship's monitors had stopped working. The good news was that the Levi was seaworthy and the engines were strong due to the retrofitting and updating Captain James had insisted upon. It had been a truly life-saving choice. The food supplies were minimal at best as a lot had been blown out of the ship and much had spoiled. There were a few loaves of Challah bread and some leaven bread; all the island fruit and coconuts had survived in the upper coolers. By another miracle, the *Levi's* clean water resources had been protected and there should be more than enough to complete the journey if all went well and we were not too far off course. While most of the crew readied for travel, Andrew and John knew it was time for some fishing. Sadie agreed and headed port side with them. The crew soon had more fish than we needed. We were now in a position to continue our journey. We knew one of our lines of communication was prayer. The crew was well versed in this and working on other ways to communicate.

All communication to the outside had been cut off due to the storm; the majority of all cell and satellite equipment – including our radios – had been destroyed or saturated beyond repair by the rogue wave. The ship could be navigated, the engines were working, but all of the instruments had been destroyed. The fuel indicators were also nonfunctional. Some of the food had to be put overboard for health reasons. The good news was that the ship remained seaworthy.

Faith and the ancient methods of navigation would be our current way home. I believed that working in harmony and unity with the gifts and skills we had, we would complete our mission and our return journey. We were confident that Clayton and the other base land team members were mounting a rescue of some kind as it had been several days since we had communicated with them. We believed in our land team and a solid emergency plan was in place for them to do everything in their power to establish communication with us and determine our location.

We only needed to determine how far off course we were. Once that assessment had been made, we would move toward home quickly. It was determined that Captain James had stayed the course. It was becoming more clear that he had sacrificed his life to give each of us a chance to live and return safely home. It was time for one last tribute to our fallen captain.

Peter, in the line of succession would now become the captain and was a true leader in every sense; very gifted, well skilled, and an individual whom we all learned to love and believed in fully. It would require each of us working in unity and with the divine help to make the journey home. We heard a loud shout from a crew member, "*Levi*, bring us home!"

In the warmth of the sun and with the smell of the brisk, salt air and a much calmer sea, the *Levi* broke through the cresting waves. It felt good to have the trade winds upon us. As I looked over the crew, I smiled with relief as the ship carried us forward. I took a moment to look down at Sadie, and for the first time in a while, I saw a face of contentment and a wagging tail. I thought about how grateful I was to have Sadie by my side when I felt her tail hit my leg as she bounded across the deck with her puppy dog eyes and a joyful grin.

We broke the waves at record speed. Smiles began to return to the faces of the crew.

Each of us had been the recipients of miracles. We'd each received a strength well beyond our own and as I looked at each crew member, the apparent glow and insight of that strength was made clear. They appeared to glow. I believe they each carried a piece of our former captain within their souls. That was true for me as well. I wondered if Captain James had taken a piece of each of us with him.

As we continued to progress on our journey, there was a feeling of excitement to return to those whom we loved and those we missed and who had supported us on our quest. With the occasional ocean sprays and the magnificent hues of the ocean and the warmth of the sun, it was not only healing but invigorating.

Dr. Bowcutt, Nathaniel, and I spent a few hours scouring the ship and going through all the smart technology and the cell phones in our possession. In doing so, we determined that the radios and other communication equipment were damaged beyond repair. No email, cell service, or other device was working. Then, in what could have been one of our darkest nights, another miracle appeared. The gift we had given Captain James, a state-of-the-art satellite watch, was found in his cabin. It was still sealed in the original package. It was dry and appeared undamaged. Even though it needed a charge, it could be the answer to our prayers. Since there was no way to reduce the ship's current load, Dr. Bowcutt and Nathaniel began to assemble an organic battery out of a fresh cut piece of island citrus fruit and a few pieces of copper and zinc from the ancient treasures we had unearthed. Only by combining ancient history and science with modern technology, were we able to communicate with our land team members.

Waiting to see if there would be success, I took Sadie up to the bow to check on Captain Peter. To my amazement, he was in tears, not of sadness but of elation for all that was good in that moment. He told me that he had taken a moment to reflect on how the hand of life and providence had been with each of us. He said he felt certain that the best was yet to come.

With that sweet moment, I returned to Dr. Bowcutt and Nathaniel to find both of them with sheepish grins. As I approached them, they indicated that we could send a message and that the GPS program was also working. From what they could tell, the crew had done an excellent job navigating the *Levi* and the crew members were definitely on the right path.

I asked Dr. Bowcutt to text out an SOS to our land crew and send them our GPS coordinates. In mere seconds – that nevertheless felt like a lifetime – we received a simple but very comforting message. It read, "Have received your message. Have received your GPS coordinates. We have shared your location with the rescuing parties. Godspeed and our prayers are with you. What is the status of the crew?" We wrote back that all crew members had been accounted for and all, but Captain James, had survived the storm. Then came the response with the information on the size and strength of the storm. We were told that it was only by a miracle that we were able to survive such a storm! Then another message told us that food, help, and supplies were on their way. A helicopter from a military ship a few hours out would be making a survival drop of additional food, communication equipment, and water so that we could stay the course.

We replied, "Crew of the Levi, looking forward to the rescue party making the survival drop. We are grateful."

Home base replied, "I am sure you have realized you are never alone."

It wasn't long before we could see the military helicopter heading in our direction. A few cheers went up and a feeling of gratitude came rolling over each of us as the rescue drop was completed. The gift of rescue taught us never to be prideful or to think that you would not need rescue. There are untold blessings in each scenario.

We ate breakfast together and talked about each of our lives; what we had done before this voyage and what we planned to do after. We formed more complete pictures of each of us, recognizing that we are more than what we do; our lives are deep and rich and this voyage was but one part of our collective and individual life journeys. We shared how the voyage had been a blessing and how the adversity we had faced had changed each of us for the better. As time permitted, I was able to continue to learn and visit with each of the crew members. They were each chosen leaders in their respective fields and shared with me that the journey and the experiences had provided them with an opportunity for growth. They felt that they shared a deeper understanding with James and each other.

Captain Peter, now at the helm, let out a shout of excitement and John was quick to point in the direction he was looking and exclaim, "Have you seen that blue whale? It has been with us ever since we laid James to rest."

This beautiful, blueish-grey, magnificent creature was always a safe distance away. It gave us a feeling of comfort with the sounds of the breaking waves and the occasional bird calls. This creature stayed with us day and night and set the pace for our journey. It wasn't difficult to believe that someone had sent the whale to guide us home.

In the illuminating starry evening, the reflection of the bright white moon shimmered on the ocean water. After speaking with each crew member, I found myself in a present moment, gazing upon the creations of the vast galaxies and numerous stars. I was overcome by the magnificent beauty of it all. I thought about how life can take you to the darkest places and raise you to a place of indescribable beauty. And in that night was another gift; the gift of additional healing and understanding. I love how nature can do that.

If the current pace continued, we were only three days from port and even though I was as excited as the crew, I found myself contemplating and meditating on the courage and the words I would need to share with James' family. To me, this would be more difficult than the journey and passing through an overwhelming storm. I kept thinking of the many gifts and stories James had shared with each of us. I remembered one story in particular from when he was a young captain.

The last night at sea was difficult for me; I couldn't help but reflect upon the loss of our beloved captain—someone who had survived so much adversity. I remembered his story of how one of his ships had capsized, but how everyone had survived. In a short time, I would have to explain to his family how this incredible individual who had faced many storms had been taken by a couple of rogue waves. This was not part of the dream I'd had when I began this journey; but when the time came, I would share the truth of Captain James, my friend, mentor, and teacher, and tell his family how he refused to back down. James had stayed the course even through one of the most challenging storms of our lives and we believed that some of his gifts were that of endurance and tenacity, as he had brought us out of harm's way.

That was the best I could do. The fact that we'd been up against unusual sea conditions had allowed the crew to discover who we truly were when faced with adversity. Captain Peter said, "we would never be the same," and I could already tell that he was right. The day was nearly over when Captain Peter came up to me and said, "It will be all right. There were fifteen of us who left and fourteen of us returning to port."

With that thought, I heard Matthew's voice call out, "Christian, you need to see this." As I headed over to see what all the noise was about, I saw several of the crew smiling. Mathew opened his hands and I saw he held a scruffy grey and white cheeked sparrow, nest and all. I was a little taken back and asked Matthew where this traveler had come from. Matthew shared with each of us that he would periodically hear a slight chirping and found the sparrow's nest with the bird and the eggs intact inside the crow's nest that had broken off during the storm. To think this very small creature and her offspring had survived such a storm. Matthew then replied, "If the sparrow and her little ones had been spared in such a storm, the sparrow must have a greater purpose as each of us surely must."

The next afternoon, we were greeted by an escort. For the final twelve hours, the escort charted the path to follow, as the majestic blue whale began to disappear into the deep blue sea. The whale had fulfilled a measure of its creation and proved to be a great comfort to each of us. There was now a white, gold, and brown bald eagle om the same path we were heading.

The crew prepared the ship for port. The storms had subsided and there was a light wind. The thought of stepping onto solid ground gave me a feeling of some peace. The time went by slowly, but we were grateful for it. The last hour was upon us and land was in sight. We were all ready for family, friends, and dry land.

As we came into port, I saw all the families gathered, even the family of Captain James, whom I hoped to comfort. I was comforted to know that all of the families would be well taken care of. Captain James had things in order with the insurance that Edwin requested. And with his share of the treasure, his family would be all right in a temporal sense. I looked over the crowd and saw Edwin, who looked relieved. And then, to my surprise, standing next to Edwin was someone I recognized. It was Ocean, the waitress from Café Ostar. I realized that I had thought of her periodically throughout the journey because I remembered what Edwin had said about her studies. Of course, I wouldn't be completely truthful if I didn't also admit that I'd thought of her when I looked deep into the crystal depths of the sea and saw the exact color of her captivating eyes. I was glad to see her again.

The ship came to a complete stop. Dry land was only a few steps away; the crew were the first to put their feet on dry and solid ground. There were cheers, applause, hugs, tears, and handshakes. I could feel the eyes of our friends and family upon me. I approached the captain's family first. Captain James' wife, Elizabeth was holding an envelope and she began to cry when she saw me. She told me she had received the news of her husband's death a couple of days ago and was deeply saddened by the loss. I reached out and gave Elizabeth a comforting hug and in return, both her daughters Grace and Serena hugged me; it was a surreal moment. Grace took a deep breath and said, "About a month prior to the voyage, my father had a routine physical and the results had come back but my dad had not opened the envelope. It was in the top right-hand drawer of his desk; my mother opened it, read it, and learned that his cancer was back. He had sixty to ninety days left at best." She smiled and said with tears in her eyes, "This journey made it possible for him to continue to do what he loved until the end."

I, too, was in tears and a relief came over me in the knowledge that Captain James had a higher purpose.

I looked off into the distance to dry my tears. Edwin was walking toward me, Ocean at his side, and I saw a small white winged dove perched and cooing in the tree behind them. A sense of peace came over me. Grace and Serena, as well as Elizabeth each gave me one more hug. I felt gratitude for what they had shared with me.

Edwin and Ocean approached. Edwin shook my hand, and said, "Well done!" He gestured to Ocean, "You remember Ocean?"

"Of course," I said, suddenly feeling somewhat shy. "It's wonderful to see you again."

"This is amazing!" she gushed. "Edwin told me about your trip and what you've discovered and what you've been through and…" she trailed off in her excitement. "You'll have to tell me everything!"

I smiled, charmed by her excitement. "It's a date," I said, suddenly bold.

Edwin smiled at that and handed me a small wooden chest. "Captain James instructed me to give this to you if he did not return." He stepped back and said, "Christian, you will go down in history!" I began to share with him what we'd found when he said, "Let's discuss that later. What did you learn?"

I glanced at Ocean and saw that she was also listening with rapt attention.

"A lifetime of knowledge and wisdom," I said. "I felt that Captain James, and Captain Peter, and each crew member had shared with me some of their gifts and pearls and in so doing, it had strengthened my foundation and forever blessed me with an inner desire to continue to learn and seek righteous knowledge and wisdom. We shared with each other the blessings of the gifts we each have."

"Yes," he said. "Do you remember the conversation we had about gifts?"

"I do," I said. How could I have forgotten? All of this was possible because Edwin had shared his gifts with me and in so doing, he was allowing me to share mine with others. "Edwin, I have nothing but gratitude for all that you have done."

"Christian," he said, "in this life, we should be forever learning. That is how we nourish the deep roots that carry us through the storms of life and give us the strength to help others and overcome the things we cannot change. We seek happiness and joy upon the path we call life. Remember, as we have discussed before, when we serve others that is when we find our true selves."

"Edwin," I replied, "my heart is full and what I have learned from each crew member – and from you – will be with me for eternity. It is truly amazing how we can acquire a multitude of gifts if we seek them for a higher or righteous purpose and if we are willing to give in return. I found it most interesting that the gifts, when combined with the right assemblage and network can have infinite value."

"Yes, you are beginning to see the right path," Edwin said, smiling. "Do you still have the pearl you received from the inspired oyster so many months ago?"

"Yes, I do," I said. I put my right hand in my pocket and withdrew the pearl I had kept with me ever since that life-changing night on the beach. I was overtaken with amazement as I reflected on this incredible gift, it seemed to shimmer and glow. Ocean's mesmerizing eyes widened at the sight.

The pearl of many moons ago. My eyes filled with tears, for I did not have the words to speak. Edwin put his hand on my shoulder and said, "As we truly begin to see, we realize that some of the most valuable treasures are those you love and those who love you. They are the people who help you magnify your gifts and help you to use them to serve and champion others. *These* are the true pearls of prosperity. Captain James returned with honor. Remember, Christian, time is also a gift. Let your life be one of honor as well."

"I can't possibly tell you how much I've learned," I said. "And more than that, I am filled with the desire to give back and to – as you so wisely put it – invest in others." I glanced at Ocean and smiled. "To help them fulfill their promise."

"That's what I like to hear," Edwin said. "Often, when people become successful or prosperous in the traditional sense of the word, they think they should be the ones doing the teaching, but I think, in fact, the opposite is true. We should always seek wisdom and search for hidden knowledge, especially from those who are not often consulted."

"I once heard that wisdom is knowledge plus time," I said.

"Ooo," Ocean chimed in, "I like that."

"And it's undoubtedly true," Edwin said. "We can have all the knowledge in the world, but without experience – which comes with time – we'll never be truly wise. That's one of the greatest pearls there is," he said, nodding at my pocket where the pearl rested. "Along the way, we learn humility as well, and we learn how to ask for help, and in so doing, we have experiences and knowledge becomes wisdom."

"And it's our job to pay it forward," I said. "To fulfill the measure of our creation by passing along that knowledge and investing in others."

"Exactly," Edwin smiled.

"There's something I've noticed," Ocean said. Edwin and I both turned to her, eager to hear what she had to say. I so appreciated that this young woman, who was just starting to make her way in the world was unafraid to speak up and make her mark. I think I saw what Edwin had seen in her when he'd first decided to invest in her; she was truly extraordinary.

"You talk about prosperity," Ocean said, "but I think you mean something different than what most people mean when they use that word."

"I do," Edwin nodded.

Ocean continued. "You aren't talking about financial prosperity – or at least not only financial prosperity. What you mean is both success and a life in which you can thrive, and the freedom to do the work that matters. One of the things – the most invaluable things – you need, is to surround yourself with others who want to do good. You bring your gifts to the common goal, and they bring theirs. And together you work in unity towards something great. If you work in sync, things happen faster. That way everyone prospers. Prosperity is a state of mind. It's like a tiny pearl you can hold onto and carry into everything you do."

"Well said, Ocean," Edwin said, smiling. "Seems like intuition is one of your gifts." Ocean beamed in response.

Edwin reached over and gave me one of his traditional hugs. He said, "We will meet up soon. Get some rest. You're going to need it with the treasure you have found. I will be introducing you to a few professionals in wealth preservation and management. "Ocean," he said, turning to her, "I hope you'll be free to join Christian in these meetings? I think someone with your expertise will be incredibly valuable to have around."

"I would be honored," Ocean said, clearly surprised.

Edwin turned back to me. "Safe travels, and from my heart, Christian, I am proud of you. You have suffered a great loss but with the gift of courage and divine strength, you and your crew prevailed."

I took a few moments and visited with a few of the other crew members and their families. Then, I found myself sitting next to the tree that was filled with a few more doves. I picked up the oak chest I had been given. As I opened it, I saw inside there were three scrolls. I reached in, took one out, and as I unrolled it, I realized it was a map of another phantom island that James had possibly discovered in his years of oceanic exploration. A feeling of inspiration came over me. The smell of vanilla began to permeate my sinuses and I soon found myself back in the present moment. There was an inscription on the inside of the oak chest which read, "Opportunities are there for those who believe."

"Ocean!" I called out. She turned from where she had been talking with Captain James's wife. I gestured for her to come see what I had. When she approached, I held the scroll out to her. "Up for an adventure?" I asked.

"I thought you'd never ask," she said, with a smile.

God can take the impossible
and make it possible.

"And the twelve gates were twelve pearls; each one of the gates was of one pearl: and the street of the city was pure gold, as if it were transparent glass."

Revelation 21:21

ACKNOWLEDGEMENTS

A huge blessing of gratitude
for my touchstone parents, Julia, Fern, Elaine, and George
for a lifetime of love and support,
for reading and sharing adventures, art, and
great books and music with me.
And for their insightful guidance and
direction along with the other villagers.

Eternal love for my wife and children
for their infinite love, encouragement, inspiration, and strength.
They humble me every day and never cease to make me proud
with the way they use their gifts.

To the artists, mentors, teachers,
business leaders, and medical professionals who invest in others
and make a difference for good while on this journey called life.

To my publisher for believing in me and for
their patience so a dream could become a reality.

To my tireless agent for her dedication and resolve and
for always keeping my best interests in mind.

To the grateful eight: Chel, Kbow, Jimi, Dody, Wass,
Mary, GG, Scooter; for all they've done for me –
and for humankind – I am forever grateful.

And to my very gifted Boston-based editor, Kristen L. Weber, who
took the journey of *Pearls for Prosperity* with me and whose
encyclopedic baseball knowledge made me feel like an MVP. Her
contributions and friendship have been truly invaluable.

Above all, my thanks to our infinite Creator, his Son, and the
beauty of His creation, without which none of this is possible.

Pearls for Prosperity

A treasure map for success, peace and genuine living, Pearls for Prosperity takes you on a journey of self discovery and generosity. Chart your own course to prosperity with this rousing adventure.

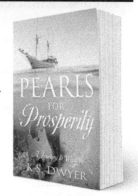

Poetry for Peace

K.S. Dwyer presents a collection of inspirational poems about life's experiences-both the everyday and the extraordinary - and how one's perspective can encourage wholeness and peace.

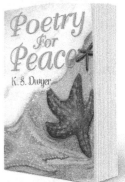

The Blue Baboon

Every time Christian's friends come over to play, his room ends up looking like a jungle. Christian says it's the Blue Baboon, his giant imaginary friend, but is this a tale too tall to be believed? When Christian insists that his primate playmate is the culprit, only the sweetest of solutions can save the day.

ABOUT THE AUTHOR

The son of a Bronze Star and Purple Heart Soldier who was killed in action when K.S. was four, KS is a Gold Star son and family member who comes from humble beginnings. He recognized early in life the importance of having great mentors and learning from great teachers, and doing everything he can to mentor and serve others. Throughout his career, KS has been an entrepreneur and a business magnate for a variety of companies including bootstrap start-ups and public and private organizations in the education, entertainment, professional sports, and financial fields.

Having served at various times as co-founder, president, CEO, and Chairman of the Board for several companies, KS has never forgotten the importance of being associated with gifted individuals in all facets of life. A firm believer in the words of Winston Churchill, "Success is not final; failure is not fatal: it is the courage to continue that counts," KS believes that both success and failure give us the opportunity to gain knowledge and wisdom, as well as a chance to grow. When not working or writing, KS spends time with his family at the ocean, boarding in a kaleidoscopic barrel wave, boating, biking, horseback riding, or contemplating the rhythms of life at a baseball game – one of the places he considers to be a house of hope and healing. KS also enjoys exploration – especially of islands – or any place where he can be at one with nature. In all he does, he seeks solace and wisdom.

CPSIA information can be obtained
at www.ICGtesting.com
Printed in the USA
BVHW030543130123
656051BV00006B/48